Praise for *Moving Foreword*

"This is the most clever book I've ever read or my name isn't Steve Martin."
—Brian Kiley, comedian and writer for *Conan*

"Very smartly done. This is possibly the best collection of funny, insightful, and entertaining forewords to books you wish were real!"
—Greg Sestero, *New York Times* bestselling coauthor of *The Disaster Artist*

"Now that Jon has come up with an idea this simple and great, he's after my investors for a chain of movie theatres that only show trailers."
—Rob Barnett, former senior executive at MTV and VH1 and former president of programming for CBS Radio

"This book is not for the illiterate."
—Alan Zweibel, former *Saturday Night Live* writer and Thurber Prize–winning author of *The Other Shulman*

"What do John Oates, Moby, Shirley Manson, and original Batman Adam West have in common? Apparently they all have or had a jones for writing introductions to books, and *Moving Foreword* indulges them in that merry fantasy. Even though the tomes they're writing about don't actually exist, the humor, cleverness, and creativity these musicians, actors, and celebs bring to the table makes you wish they did."
—David Browne, author, *Fire and Rain: The Beatles, Simon & Garfunkel, James Taylor, CSNY, and the Lost Story of 1970*

"Ah, the all-important foreword. They always remind me of the *utter* import of every introduction I hear the emcee make just before I take the stage as a stand-up comedian. Sure, the audience paid damn good money to see me, and they did it in advance. (Many had to get a babysitter at no small additional fee.) So it always matters that the words that the emcee chooses are just the right amount, and in the right order. The objective is to impress them before I take the stage—just the same as with a foreword. Remind the reader that they were correct to have made the effort to buy the book. That they are smart to have chosen this book among the sea of literary options. Fill them with the confidence of the best version of themselves. It's a total affirmation that they made the right choice . . . this time. Well, this is a whole book of perfect introductions to acts you'll never hear."

—Kevin Pollak, actor and comedian

"If one thing is certain in the book business, it's that nothing tops a good foreword. Especially if it's from someone famous. And I don't mean the shitty kind of famous, where only teenagers at the mall recognize you because they saw your face on a YouTube end credits screen once. I mean really famous. Famous Famous. The kind of fame where you can have people follow you around the world, throwing peanuts at your enemies, which is the kind of thing I hear Angelina Jolie does. Anyway, what was this for again?"

—B.J. Mendelson, author of *Social Media Is Bullshit*

MOVING
FOREWORD

MOVING FOREWORD

Real Introductions to Totally Made-Up Books

Edited by
JON CHATTMAN

BenBella Books, Inc.
Dallas, TX

Copyright © 2019 by Jon Chattman
Foreword copyright © 2019 by Rainn Wilson
"Pizzazz: The Life and Genius of Darrell Hammond" (page 12) copyright © 2019 by Darrell Hammond
"The Lure of the Flies" (page 161) copyright © 2019 by Adam West

BenBella

BenBella Books, Inc.
10440 N. Central Expressway, Suite 800
Dallas, TX 75231
www.benbellabooks.com
Send feedback to feedback@benbellabooks.com

Printed in the United States of America
10 9 8 7 6 5 4 3 2 1

Library of Congress Cataloging-in-Publication Data is available upon request.
ISBN 9781946885814 (paper over board)
ISBN 9781948836197 (electronic)

Editing by Claire Schulz and Leah Wilson
Copyediting by Miki Alexandra Caputo
Proofreading by James Fraleigh and Jenny Bridges
Text design by Publishers' Design and Production Services, Inc.
Text composition by PerfecType, Nashville, TN
Author photo by Lindsay Burdick Witts
Printed by Lake Book Manufacturing

Distributed to the trade by Two Rivers Distribution, an Ingram brand
www.tworiversdistribution.com

Special discounts for bulk sales (minimum of 25 copies) are available. Please contact bulkorders@benbellabooks.com.

For my "three little birds,"
Noah, Zachary, and Lila,
who always keep me moving forward.

Contents

Foreword

"**W**AIT. You want me to write a *foreword* to a book about *forewords*?!"

That's what I said when my friend Jon called me to ask about writing this piece. "Cool! Count me in," I said. Then, switching gears, I put on my best Dwight Schrute hat and said, "Well, how much are you willing to pay me to do it?"

Then Jon was like, "How about *you* pay *me* for the privilege, asshat? I mean, you're a mostly unemployed former sitcom actor, you should be kissing our asses to be a part of this one-of-a-kind literary event."

I thought about it a second and then, ashamed, red-faced, I croaked, "How does $800 sound?"

Jon was like, "We'll take it. But whatever you write better be good or you're finished. FINISHED, I SAY!"

I gulped fearfully, wrote Jon a personal check, and here we are!

Being a part of one of the most "meta" books in human history cost me $800, untold hours of writing time, and buttloads of self-esteem. I hope you like it! (Please like it. Because I will be contractually forced to pay an additional thirty-seven dollars for each negative Amazon review. Please like it.)

So, a foreword about forewords. Where does one begin? I know, let's go back into the world of *history*! To ancient Rome!

The very first foreword ever written was composed in the year 237 by Landula Henthrius, a minor Roman senator and historian of infamous gladiator deaths, who begged his friend Lupitius Golumnus, author of *Trident Eviscerations Made Easy*, to be allowed to write a *libro ante libro* or "book *before* the book." Landula had experimentally eviscerated several of his slower, older slaves in grotesque ways using his cousin Festus's gladiator trident that he had found in the back of the chariot garage. As this was before YouTube, he wanted to share his gruesome findings with a wider audience than just his wife, children, and Festus.

The only extant copy includes Landula's diagrams for some intricate disemboweling techniques to which he had given such nicknames as the "Gut Plucker," the "Penis Zipper," and "Get Quickly to the Stomach."

Apparently, the book sold like candy and "anyone who was anyone" carried around this bestseller with the logo of a bloody trident on the cover. It was like *The Girl on the Train* or *Who Moved My Cheese?* of the third century. And it made literary superstars of the authors Landula and Lupitius, who gave readings and live demonstrations throughout the empire, disemboweling hundreds of actual slaves before adoring crowds.

Our story comes to a tragic end, however, when Landula, after a drunken argument, was himself eviscerated *a collum ad coles* (from throat to cock) by none other than his cousin Festus, a notorious alcoholic.

What a way to go, though, amirite? A trident to the gut!? So effin' rad!

Switching gears. In life there are some things one simply cannot underestimate: wolverines, gastroenteritis, and the importance of forewords. One can also never underestimate the vast difference between a foreword, an introduction, and a preface. (If you don't know the difference, something is probably very, very wrong with you or you are an idiot. At least that is what my friend Jon told me when I asked.)

So, let me fill you in. A preface is for when the book is really lame and complicated, and the author needs to tell you why he even wrote the book he's just written. An introduction is for when the book is really lame and complicated, and the author needs to tell you what's inside the rest of the book. A foreword is for when a book is not going to sell very well and the author needs a currently unemployed former sitcom actor to write something, *anything*, in a desperate, sweaty attempt to stick his "has-been" name on it and sell more copies.

Forewords (*fore* plus *words*, or the words before a book) are also not to be confused with forward (the direction) or forwards (like in basketball). (I highly doubt that Blake Griffin or Charles Barkley would know what a foreword was if it bit them on the high top.) And, fun fact, "forword" is not a word at all.

Now! To the book at hand. Perhaps, dear reader, you enjoy browsing through tomes at your local independent bookstore and flipping open the vibrant cover to land on your favorite part, the foreword. Perhaps you read a bit of it right there in the aisle, to get a general sense of the very book you're holding in your hand and, sold by the foreword author's promises, bring the book home—where you realize the book itself is a disappointment.

Well, no more! With this book, you don't have to suffer through the rest of the book. There is no rest of the book. We've taken the best bit of any book and made an even bigger book out of it. It's a book of best bits! What you're reading is the book equivalent of eating the frosting off a cake. This book is all tantalizing foreplay without any of the tedious complications of sex! It's a baseball game of constant homeruns and none of those endless periods where guys adjust gloves and jockstraps and spit and talk to each other on the mound. It's like the flavor-rich first two minutes of chewing gum! You get the idea.

So get ready to stick a fork into some sticky, gooey goodness— tales of love and lust, humor, mystery, and the exploits of Hollywood elite like the Kool-Aid Man and Chewbacca. Enter a world in which Central Perk doesn't only serve up coffee—it dishes out murder. Go forward like a power forward into the fantastical land of FOREWORDS!

Rainn Wilson

Introduction

MERRIAM-WEBSTER'S COLLEGIATE DICTIONARY defines a foreword as "prefatory comments (as for a book) especially when written by someone other than the author." Surprisingly for a reference book, that sounds pretty vague, so I'll try to elaborate on the old standby's inadequate definition.

A foreword gets you buckled up and ready before you take a literary journey. It's the run-up before you dive into the book. It adds some upfront zest to the flavor of the book. It paints a picture of what's to come. A good foreword is like the music piped into a theater before the lights dim and the concert starts. Yes, forewords set the stage for the show to come. They come in all shapes and sizes, some extending for pages and others for just a few paragraphs. They can be personal, reflective, celebratory, funny, insightful, gut punching, playful, serious, or all of the above.

Indeed, a foreword is most often written by someone other than the author. To name just a few notable examples, Keith Hernandez wrote a foreword for former New York Mets teammate Mookie Wilson; Elvis Costello wrote a foreword for Loretta Lynn; and Bill Clinton has written forewords to at least six published books, including Nelson Mandela's *In His Own Words* (I guess even former presidents need hobbies that extend beyond golf and paid public speeches). Forewords often attempt to provide some insight into what's going on inside the author's mind. They offer stories and anecdotes from the author's friends or testimonials from colleagues in the same field. It's like an endorsement, something to build up the author's credibility, or to get readers interested in an author they might not have read before. In the case of a medical book, an expert in the field might weigh in on the importance of the subject matter. For a cookbook, a fellow chef might emphasize the importance of healthy dishes. In the case of an autobiography, often another celebrity kicks off the show. Foreword writers usually want to pay tribute to someone they love or admire—perhaps also to gently rib them or reminisce.

The celebrity hook was partly the inspiration for this book. The beginnings of the idea came to me after my experiences publishing my previous works of literature. (I say "literature," though my books include an ode to celebrity mustaches and an homage to wrestlers in spandex, so pardon me if I've taken liberties with the term.) I have been fortunate to have an amazing roster of people—including musician John Oates (featured in this book), WWE Hall of Famer Mick Foley, and former MLB pros Fred Lynn and Kevin Millar—write forewords for my books. I remember leaping for joy when they gave me their respective thumbs-up. The inclusion of a celebrity foreword instantly adds a stamp of approval to your work.

Even with all the effort that goes in to securing (and writing!) a really killer foreword, it must be said that most of the time readers care more about, you know, the book itself. The foreword's nice and all, but it's not *usually* why we're there.

So why *this* book? Why forewords to books that don't exist? Well, it must also be said that even though forewords aren't often the main reason for picking up a book, forewords can often end up surpassing the books themselves. Sometimes they're so well written and hype up the book so much that it actually takes away from what you're about to read and crushes its mojo. Like a captivating trailer to a film that turns out to be a dud, the buildup is just that—a buildup. The end result may actually be a great letdown. Just ask *The Last Jedi* trolls.

Since the best parts of books are often the parts before the books themselves, I present this work of "literature" to you. It takes the fun of books but leaves out the book part. Think of this as licking the icing off a whole pack of Oreos without having to bother about the soggy cookie part. I wanted this book to be as exciting as a great foreword, but I didn't want you to have to sit through a whole book afterward. (Who has the time anymore to sit down and read a Tolkien-sized quest nowadays? There's a reason graphic novels sell so well. Blood! Guts! Action, baby! No dull descriptions of landscape to slow things down. And quick dialogue!) We live in a world of immediacy and forewords are as fast and furious as Vin Diesel, so let's just keep the good stuff.

I wanted to bring together an anthology of talent, and showcase a variety of funny, creative, and thought-provoking writing.

The prompt was simple: provide a real foreword to a fake book with full creative freedom, just a little guidance. But it wasn't an easy task. Remember, people often want to write forewords for friends or people they *admire*. I, on the other hand, consider myself a Z-list celebrity. My friends don't exactly walk the red carpet (and though I've taken some friends down a few of them, the question that follows us is usually not "Who are you wearing?" but "Who are you, again?"). So, initially, pitching this book was met with a lot of *Huh?*s, *Say whaaa?*s, and *Um, I don't get it*s by many publicists, agents, and managers. It was also met with a lot of *That's such a great idea, but no*s and *I'm sorry, can you please explain this again?*s. At one point, I even approached Alf,* that '80s icon and lover of cats, only to hear, "At the risk of sounding too forward, my honest reply is to say I would not be looking forward to writing a foreword. With that being said, moving forward, I wish you the best of luck with your project!"

But, many people did get it, the project took off, and the brilliant forewords in this book embody that vision. You're about to read more than sixty forewords written by an array of talent from all walks of pop life, from television and film personalities to singer-songwriters to journalists and everyone in between. Their entries are surprising, funny, spine-tingling, intentionally confusing, and a boatload of other

---

*My editor, who's a total killjoy, is making me tell you that it wasn't *really* Alf. It was Paul Fusco, the creator and voice actor behind the character. But he really did say that. (Best. Rejection. Ever.)

cool adjectives. Somehow this eclectic mix of tales comes together to create the best fake book you'll ever read.*

Across chapters covering everything from sex to music to science, you'll read forewords that introduce you to a tween bible, a murder mystery by a "Garbage" icon, fly-fishing from the original Batman, a guide to improv, and arguably the best thing Sir Ian McKellen has ever written (well, he didn't actually write it, but still . . .). You'll laugh. You'll cry. You will question the importance of your boogers. And, you will do so in bite-sized, golden-nugget short stories. This isn't Tolstoy. You won't have to dedicate months of your life to carefully analyzing the text. Whether you're on a plane or in the crapper, this book is for you. Read it in one sitting or pick and choose from different chapters. By all means, take a page from House of Pain and "jump around."

So, toss away your big books, and jump into this meta concept. In an age where the phrase "fake news" has been used to death, let's embrace forewords to fake books. Wherever you are, cozy up and enjoy the ride!

---

*Well, one clarification. The books are fake, but . . . some of the content is super fake, and some is only kinda fake. Many of the contributors have written as themselves, more or less; some of them have layered fake on fake and have written these *as someone else*. That said, there's some #realtalk here, including the exploits of a real 1970s game show host, some insanely insensitive quotes from the late Christopher Hitchens, and a New Kid's ill-fated stint as an emu farmer. And all that stuff, believe it or not, is real. (Definitely too real for the emus.)

Biography, Autobiography, and Memoir

WRITING WITH THE STARS

THROUGHOUT THE HISTORY OF TIME (or *Time* magazine, anyway), we've been obsessed with celebrities. Ah, celebrities . . . we can't get enough of them, whether following them on Instagram, watching them rise or free fall on TMZ, or reading books about them. And, some of the best forewords come before a celebrity biography or memoir. Typically, a bio will start out with a strong, often poignant foreword by a friend or longtime admirer. For example, for his autobiography, the late Burt Reynolds had pal and *Deliverance* costar Jon Voight pen his foreword. We're unclear what Dom DeLuise was doing that day, but let's move on. In his book *Scalia Speaks*, the late Supreme Court Justice Antonin Scalia had Ruth Bader Ginsburg lend the foreword. And wrestling legend the Iron Sheik was selected by Margaret "the Iron Lady" Thatcher for her memoir. (That last one is totally not true, but we can only dream about what that would've been like.) Anyway, with that, we bring you a series of introductions to celebrity chronicles we wish we could open but can't, because, you know, this entire book is fake.

WHITNEY MATHESON is a writer who appreciates pop culture and fruity beverages. Read more of her work at whitneymatheson.com.

Foreword to Kool-Aid Man's *Bustin' Through: Confessions of a Kool-Aid Man*

By Whitney Matheson

ABOUT THREE YEARS AGO, my dear friend Kool-Aid Man and I were strolling through Central Park, reminiscing about the time he rescued Liza Minnelli from a swarm of angry bumblebees.

"K-AM," I said, nudging his handle. "Your stories are so amazing. Ever think about writing a book?"

In your hands are the juicy fruits of his labor, *Bustin' Through: Confessions of a Kool-Aid Man*. Told in 132 exhilarating chapters, it's the brave and revealing journey of a guy who went from a flavorless and lonely childhood to busting through walls.

Here, K-AM divulges the details behind his well-known triumphs, like becoming a world-famous mascot by the age of twenty-five and romancing everyone from Swiss Miss to a (much older) Mrs. Butterworth. By the late '70s, he was—literally and figuratively—bigger than Elvis.

But make no mistake, this pitcher-shaped pitchman has lived through dark times, too. In chapter thirty-two, he opens up about his ongoing struggle with gingivitis. In chapter fifty-five, we finally hear his perspective on the time he crashed through the wall of an Iowa City police station (and his resulting six-month stint in anger management). Then, of course, there were the high-stakes poker games with the Nesquik Rabbit and Hawaiian "Punchy" Punch, leaving him nearly bankrupt in the late '90s.

"Most people see me as a full pitcher," he confided to Oprah Winfrey in a now-legendary 2002 interview. "But inside, I've always felt half empty."

The twenty-first century hasn't been easy for K-AM, but ultimately, he has come to terms with the changing times, emerging a more thoughtful, health-conscious hero. Today, he enjoys a modest and sugar-free life in Brooklyn, nearly unrecognizable in a slim stainless-steel carafe. He appears at conventions and events a few times a year, but mostly, he's content to be immersed in hobbies like making artisanal mustard and playing in a weekend bocce ball league.

While autograph seekers used to bombard him daily, K-AM is now happy to dissolve into mainstream society, occasionally stopping for selfies with nostalgic Generation Xers. Most are appreciative, but a few gaze at him sadly, as if to say, "Why can't you be the same person you used to be?"

Oh, yeah? Perhaps they should take a few steps closer to the man and contemplate their own blurry reflections.

Several years ago, I happened to be seated beside the liquid legend on a cross-country flight. We struck up a friendship and chatted about pop culture until we parted ways. (Fun fact: he's a Carrie with Miranda tendencies.) Today, we talk every week, and sometimes he'll recall his crazy adventures and encounters with the rich and famous. Other times we'll just discuss the humidity.

This cultural icon has left an indelible imprint on upper lips across the globe, but, as you're about to find out, so much lies beneath the surface. Grab a straw and prepare to suck down this incredible odyssey from Kool-Aid Boy to Kool-Aid Man. I assure you, the taste it'll leave in your mouth isn't merely sugar water.

It's hope.

KERSI ASARE (@ItsKersiTime) is a comedian from New York City.

Foreword to Samwell's *What What (in the Butt): The Man Behind the Booty*

By "Testas Sterone," life coach, producer, personal trainer, professor emeritus at YouTube University, and THE first viral video talent manager of all time forever and ever

B Y THE TIME you see the words WHAT WHAT emblazoned in rhinestones across his perfectly sculpted cheeks as they vibrate to the melodic beat of "What What (in the Butt)," you've already been drawn into his world. He is Samuel Johnson, better known as Samwell, and *best* known as What What (in the Butt) Guy, or WW(ITB)G™®. WW(ITB)G's landmark video took YouTube—and the universe—by storm. The track features his sensual serenading tightly coupled with sharp, witty lyrics. The visuals let the world know that he's one part Prince and one part Chris Rock. A true living legend.

That summer of 2007, I was riding shotgun on this roller coaster. Just like a man of his great stature should, WW(ITB)G had reached out for expert assistance from yours truly, and together we propelled that man's backside into the stratosphere. As he was being wined, dined, and courted by the biggest movie studios and record companies in the world, our relationship blossomed, and we became fast friends. Life was fantastic.

Who am I? Testas Sterone? Let's just say I'd be nowhere without WW(ITB)G, and those finely tuned buttocks wouldn't have even smelled outer space without a lil' boost from Sterone. Together we transformed the industry buzz surrounding "What What (in the Butt)" from a mere tidal wave into a big-ass monsoon! "What What (in the Butt)" raised the bar and was Certified Viral®, thus changing the world forever, ad infinitum. That track was hotter than Hendrix, Nelly, and Bruno Mars's hits combined! (Oh, that fire was so hot baby!)

Not enough credit is given to the folks that make the big things happen behind the scenes—unsung heroes like me. So I established synergies, made a few calls, and I am now the cofounder (and two-time winner) of the YouTube Cocontributors Award™. Because you can't spell "YouTube Sensation" without Testas Sterone, baby! Don't even try it!

Anyway, it was when our views reached into the millions that we started to get calls from Comedy Central, Showtime, Sony, and HBO. A tour ensued, with all the expected merchandise—WHAT WHAT rhinestone pants (think Hammer pants, baby!), heart and booty–shaped chocolates, and WW(ITB)G Bobble-Butt Dolls (It's that famous booty *bobblehead style*). Even Sir Mix-a-Lot's people inquired about a guest spot on "Baby Got Back 2000." And of course I got him this book deal. We got so many offers we had to start turnin' 'em down, baby! And just like that, in a whole three weeks WW(ITB)G became one of THE most outstanding entertainers of our generation. His meteoric rise assured his name will go down alongside artists and icons like Skee-Lo, the Baha Men, and Right Said Fred.

As I promised the kid, the story of our success led us right into the C-suite! During our first and last WHAT WHAT Digital Summit and Retreat Week, we rubbed elbows with CEOs and brainstormed ways to optimize WW(ITB)G's brand and further expansion into Butt, What What, and "What What (in the Butt)" related merchandise in their Fortune 500 organizations. While munching on bacon-wrapped scallops during a break in the Summit, I noticed that WW(ITB)G was giving me all of his bacon owing to his religious beliefs. Although I still have no freakin' idea what those religious beliefs *are*, his dedication to these beliefs is dwarfed only by his dedication to his booty. The butt that started it all takes on nearly three hundred squats, two hundred lunges, three hours of Zumba classes, and damn near fifteen hours of dance rehearsals per week to maintain its signature rigidity. WW(ITB)G possesses no ordinary butt—it's extraordinary. He still can't even walk down the street without someone snapping a butt selfie or giving it a nice slap to confirm its firmness (oh, he secretly loves it!). Even JLo herself; Jennifer Lopez once said that his buttocks were among the best she's ever seen in the business, buns down. Not to mention, for *me*, that derriere opened up new avenues of revenue like a Mack truck. Now I'm churning out viral hits like the Amish on butter, baby! All thanks to WW(ITB)G, his booty, and our extraordinary team.

At the 2010 YouTube Innovation Leadership Symposium Forum for Leaders and Innovators, we discussed potential areas of growth, synergies, and new revenue streams with the YouTube executive team in Palo Alto. WW(ITB)G gave a resounding and passionate speech detailing his rise to fame, his creative process, and the importance of perseverance via squat thrusts. He touched on ways to make sure his legacy lives on and pointedly asked the audience, "How can we make sure that an artist capable of another 'What What (in the Butt)' is sculpted from the next generation of America's children?"

Always humble, he signed autographs for hours and took pictures with his adoring fanbase, as any good-hearted celebrity would do.

But this would be one boring-ass book if it was all a fairy tale (plus that kind of sappy crap doesn't sell!). As we all know, WW(ITB)G's life has not been all roses and derriere-related compliments. As with any rise to fame, there was a highly publicized and politicized dark side. Plus, once we got too big, the painkillers and poppin' champagne on deluxe yachts became more important than the *work* for WW(ITB)G. And to boot, some of the things I had to do to get us to the top led to my immediate removal from my position at YouTube University (but hey—you've got to get your hands dirty if you want to play with the big dogs, baby!).

But . . . even as we grew apart and he faltered publicly, WW(ITB) G never faltered privately. His enthusiasm and drive for success never vanished. Luckily, this man possesses an astonishing set of cheeks to land on—and I learned that WW(ITB)G and that backside are absolutely forged from steel. He has bounced back like I always knew he would. Through thicc ass and thin, and even throughout his ongoing litigation against me, I've maintained the coveted title of *Awesomest Friend*. (Even though your old pal Testas Sterone isn't mentioned as much in this book as he should be, that's OK, we can negotiate our own book deals. Check out *Synergize Your Way to Stardom* by yours truly, the one, the only Testas Sterone, on shelves next year!)

After we reconciled at his YouTube Hall of Fame induction ceremony, I could see that the life of parties, award shows, drinking, after-after parties, drugs, hot-air balloon rides, and sex in said balloons (see chapter thirteen) had taken their toll on his vitality. But behind his eyes I could still see the old fire and desire to make another hit. And his ass was as tight as ever. When WW(ITB)G sauntered down the red carpet that night, everyone from the Don't Tase Me Bro to the Sneezing Panda were frozen in amazement, like they were stuck in time staring at twin Beyoncés working the runway. Even Chocolate Rain Guy remarked in his booming baritone voice, "My, those cheeks *are* exquisite." That's all I needed to know that another YouTube hit is on the horizon (Testas knows a winner when he sees one!). It's in his blood, it's in his heart, it's in his ass.

This is his story: the man, the legend, the humble beginning, the rise, the fall, the resurrection, the Butt—What What.

Break a leg—and a cheek, my friend.

DANTE MERCADANTE is the CEO (chief eating officer) for Nice Guy Tours (niceguytours.com), a New York City walking food tour company. He is also an actor and a comedian.

Foreword to Bill Pullman's
I Wasn't in Twister: A Memoir

By Dante Mercadante

B EING ASKED TO WRITE a foreword for a book is a real honor. Writing a book takes a lot of blood, sweat, and tears. Many authors treat a book like a child, putting in loads of effort, sometimes *years* of hard work. I can see why. So when you're asked to write a foreword, you're being told, "Look, I've been working really hard at this thing, and I want you to tell people what to expect."

So why would this well-established actor ask a food tour guide from New York City to pen the intro to his book?

Good question. I'll get to it.

I feel a bit of pressure here—it's kind of like being an opening act. When you're looking for the right opener, you don't want someone so amazing that they blow the headliner away, but you don't want them to stink, either. The comedian Brad Garrett—you probably know him from *Everybody Loves Raymond*—tells a funny story about opening for Frank Sinatra, something he did a couple of times early in his stand-up career. Garrett says that at the end of one of his sets opening up for Ol' Blue Eyes, he said, "Stick around, we've got a great singer coming out," or something to that effect. The Chairman, unfortunately, didn't get the joke, and needless to say, he was a little upset. Supposedly, he had some of his goons tell Mr. Garrett never to do that again. So you see, you want to be good as an opening act, but not *too* good.

It's a lot of pressure when a guy like Bill Pullman asks a regular Joe Sixpack like me to write the foreword for his book. I'm a nobody, and he's a star. He's the actor we all loved in *Weird Science* . . . or maybe it was *Independence Day*. I gotta look that up.

Anyway, I used to work in sales, and I remember my boss once advising me, "Tell them . . . Tell them you told them. Then tell them again." I think that one comes from the world of commercials. It means, like, first you have to tell them. Then, you remind them you've told them. Then, just for good measure, you tell them again. It's a way to make sure the consumer hears you and understands what you're saying.

For example, did you ever see a commercial and say to yourself, "What is this even for? Are they selling computers? Phones? Hmmmm . . . Maybe it's for that car?" That's the last thing you want to do when you're selling something. When you see one of those infomercial-type commercials, you know exactly what they are selling and what it is purported to do.

"Purported." That's a funny word. You never hear someone use the word "purport," but you sometimes hear "purported."

Anyway, sorry, I got off track there for a minute. Let's get back to why we're here.

You're about to read an exceptional book, and it's a real honor to have been chosen to write the foreword. It's something I don't take lightly. It's a big responsibility. I want to make sure I present the information to you all in such a way that is concise and easy to understand. I want to tell you about the book, but not so much that you don't even need to read it.

On the flip side, I don't want to tell you so little that you think, "What the heck is this guy even talking about? Is it a phone? A computer?" I wouldn't want that to happen. That would be so embarrassing! Because once something is printed in a book, it's part of the world forever. There is no taking it back. I would hate for the whole world to think I'm a fool who doesn't know what he's talking about.

I'm just so honored that Bill asked me to write this after we locked eyes one day at Katz's Deli on the Lower East Side. We'd never met before (and to be honest, we haven't seen each other since). But he was really cool about it when I told him I loved him in *True Lies*. And I'll always cherish the true friendship that blossomed out of our shared love of pastrami.

At least, I think that's what it was.

Bill's memoir tells a classic Hollywood tale of a character actor who never got into trouble, led a wonderful life, has a great family, and didn't star in anything with Helen Hunt. That said, it still is a page-turner with lots of twists and turns. For instance, did you know he wasn't in *Twister*? Did you know he wasn't in a movie with Dermot Mulroney or Dylan McDermott? Did you know he's not Bill Paxton, and Bill Paxton actually died in 2017 (I cried when I found that out)? Read on, and you'll learn so much more about this beloved actor.

So without further ado, I present to you *I Wasn't in Twister*, a memoir by Bill Pullman.

DARRELL HAMMOND is the second-longest-running cast member in *SNL* history. He is the author of the *New York Times* bestseller *God, If You're Not Up There, I'm F*cked*, currently being turned into a play by Tony Award–winning director Christopher Ashley. He is the current staff announcer for *SNL*, and is touring the nation with his stand-up comedy.

Foreword to Walter Isaacson's *Pizzazz: The Life and Genius of Darrell Hammond*

By the Essence of Darrell Hammond

"How 'bout a little less talk and a little more shut the fuck up?" The speaker is me, or rather *was* me, when I was alive. At the moment, I'm dead—in a casket in the ground in upstate New York. I died on December 21, 2016, in New York City at around two o'clock in the afternoon. When I heard the publishers were moving forward with this biography, I immediately reached out to every medium I could find, eventually making contact with Larry Dubois, the famed Staten Island medium. For though Walter did a fantastic job capturing my life and career, I want to tell you my own story. It's not a fancy story. It's not full of extraordinary things. It's just my simple account of the cruel twist of fate that robbed me of my one true passion—dance.

Reader, you may not believe some of what you read in the book to come, how I gave up comedy to study ballet in Moscow under Vladimir Vasiliev, and that's all right—half the time I don't believe it myself, and I'm the one who lived it.

There's one day of my life that Walter got wrong, because he had no way of knowing the truth, and that's the day I want to tell you about now—the day that changed everything.

I pulled into the parking garage underneath the New York City Ballet, where I am (or was) the lead dancer. I'm not tooting my own horn, I'm just telling you this because it pertains to the story. As I eased my car into the spot normally reserved for Darrell Hammond, I saw that my name had been removed and replaced by another.

Dora the Explorer.

I blinked at the sign, thoughts spinning in my head, and I walked over to the booth where the parking lot attendant takes your keys and gives you a stub. I said, "Um, yeah, Vinnie? What's the gag?"

"Ain't no gag. Dora the Explorer took your job, friend. It happened last night. Didn't nobody tell you? All you ever worked for in your whole lousy, miserable life belongs to her now. You're done here. Done everywhere."

Apparently when the earth is about to open underneath your feet, you hear flies buzzing in your ears. I did. Vinnie went on, "It's capitalism, my man. Ticket sales are down. Your style of doin' things, ya know, par excellence and all that, ain't cuttin' it no more with John Q. Public. These are uncertain times; people don't want craftsmanship no more. They want pizzazz. Dora the Explorer got pizzazz. You know what you got? You got nothin'. Ain't that right, Mr. D? Ain't it true you got nothin' no more?"

I say, "How 'bout a little less talk and a little more . . ." well, reader, you know the rest.

I had to admit he was right about one thing: without my role at the ballet, I had nothing.

Silence. Slow motion. The sound of a heartbeat. The sound of flies.

I walked out of the parking garage and took a right, walked to Broadway, another right, then walked to Sixty-Third Street. I stood on the corner, facing west. The light changed.

Replaced by Dora the Explorer? I like Dora as much as anybody else does, but . . . the buzzing flies drowned the rest of my thoughts.

Even if you are a fan of the one replacing you, which I was, it doesn't sting any less. Negative thoughts poured in, taking over. I said to myself, "Pretty soon I'll be forgotten . . . forgotten, but not gone."

I started to cross the street. The driver of the SUV must have thought that since the light had only just turned yellow he'd still have enough time to speed through. I never saw him. Died quick, they said, no pain or anything.

There's a lot that happened in that moment, reader, and you'll read about it in the pages to come—from the perspective of my family, my friends, and the other dancers. But there is one thing that only I—the essence of Darrell Hammond—could tell you: what it was like to die.

Now, I always loved to dance. I love the way the music shares the contents of your heart without needing words. I loved the way it made me feel—the way it lifted my spirit and the moment I could feel the audience take part in the story I told. That is why I danced, and it is these moments that hang like golden orbs in my memory, even now.

The moment I was hit by that car, all those orbs crashed over me like a wave, in one great pounding motion. In this book, I'd have liked to share these with you, reader. I'd have liked to share each orb, and tell you why it made my life the dance it was.

But now, speaking through a TV psychic, I don't have quite enough time.

I can tell you that at the very end of it all there is warmth, light, and a rising sun. Somewhere a tinkling on a piano, a harp. The wind is so clean and pure. I drifted over the Hudson River—past Tarrytown. Over the cornfields of Iowa, the Rocky Mountains, over the desert, moving over the Catalina Mountains in Arizona, moving into a world where time never began, and where it will never end. Beyond the moon, beyond the rain.

Until . . .

Plop.

The first shovelful of dirt hit my casket.

Plop. *Why was I back?*

I heard the gravediggers talking.

"Who was this guy?"

"I dunno—some kind of famous dancer or somethin'. Everybody said he was the best in the world."

Plop.

"So, what happened?"

"Oh well, guess he goes to work one day and finds out he got replaced by Wile E. Coyote."

"Can Wile E. Coyote even dance?"

A laugh.

"He don't need to—he got pizzazz."

Right.

"Yeah, the guy got so upset he walked right out into traffic. Took his own life. Fuckin' shame. They said his last words were, 'forgotten, but not gone.' Probably a fag."

"Aren't they all?"

"Most def."

They chuckled.

It's a funny feeling—realizing how you'll be remembered. Even this biography hints that I may have stepped in front of the car intentionally. There's a whole lot of life still to come after you've gone. And if you don't make sure you tell your own story . . . well, you'll be stuck with whatever anybody else says about you.

Or you can haunt the bejesus out of a Staten Island psychic until he agrees to set the record straight.

Thank you, reader, for sharing my journey with me. It means more than you could know.

Foreword to Earl Pittman, Jr.'s *Vance DeGeneris: An Unauthorized Biography*

By Vance DeGeneres

YOU'RE PROBABLY THINKING, wow, that is really odd Vance DeGeneres is writing the foreword for an unauthorized biography about Vance DeGeneres. Yes, it is odd. Mr. Pittman contacted me a couple of years ago asking to interview me for a biography he was writing about me. I politely declined; I don't think I'm anywhere near interesting enough to have a biography written about me. Mr. Pittman obviously disagreed, as evidenced by the book you're now reading. I didn't hear from him again until he sent me the finished manuscript just before publication. Mr. Pittman kindly offered me the chance to write the foreword for the book, and I accepted—under the condition that my words not be edited in any way. He agreed to that condition, and here we are.

First, let me congratulate Mr. Pittman on actually writing a book in the first place. It's not an easy feat. Before this unauthorized biography, Mr. Pittman candidly told me, he had written a novel and a children's book, neither of which was ever published. My only connection with Mr. Pittman is apparently through 23andMe. He did the genetic test and claims we're distantly related, although he's sent no documentation to prove it. You might be asking, "Why would he write a biography on you and not your more famous sister?" In fact, that was one of my very first questions to him. His reply: "While Chelsea is a funny lady, my intention is to write a series of biographies on the less-famous siblings of famous people."

Apparently, he believes my sister is Chelsea Handler. I saw no need to correct him.

I'll do my best to be kind in this foreword, but I will be honest. Not to be picky, but DeGeneres doesn't have an *i* in it. And this is not a big deal, but he claims I grew up in the French Quarter of New Orleans. Incorrect. We lived in Metairie, a suburb of New Orleans, and I earned money by mowing lawns and washing cars, not by tap dancing on street corners. I won't go into detail, because it would take too much time, but suffice it to say that much of what he wrote about my childhood is filled with inaccuracies, and some of it feels like he just made it up. If he had taken even a little bit of time to do some research, maybe talked to neighbors, he might've at least gotten it partly right. Mr. Pittman freely admitted that he just "took a stab" at guessing which grade schools I went to. (As he put it, "Nobody cares about stuff like that.")

He also had some inaccuracies regarding my parents' professions. My father was an insurance salesman, not a bagman for the Mafia. And while it's correct that my mother sold *World Book Encyclopedia*s, she was never a cheerleader for the New Orleans Saints.

He wrote several chapters about my life between my childhood and when my career started that are so boring. I have to admit I mostly skipped them, so I'm not totally sure what they're about. Some of it wasn't even about me, but if you have any interest in cheesemaking or Renaissance art, do turn your attention to chapters 12 and 15. And if he had simply done a Google search, he would've known that I was in the Marine Corps, not the Merchant Marine.

Jumping ahead to when I started my career, Mr. Pittman writes that I was part of a musical group called "Willy's Show," and that we performed mainly at strip joints on Bourbon Street. No. We were a comedy team, not a "singing duo who got their start on *American*

Idol." (Obviously . . . *American Idol* wasn't even on TV in the 1970s.) Our name was "The Mr. Bill Show," and . . . okay, we *did* perform at a strip joint on Bourbon Street, but only one time. Mr. Pittman also wrote an entire chapter on the time I spent as a political reporter and how I broke many important award-winning news stories. Totally false. I *was* a fake journalist as a correspondent on a comedy news show, but I have yet to earn a Pulitzer—let alone the Nobel.

In fact, the only chapter that didn't have any inaccuracies was a five-page chapter detailing how he had seen me eating lunch one day at a restaurant in Santa Barbara. While the level of detail on my food order and activities for the day was quite astounding, it has unfortunately required me to trigger a police investigation into his "research practices." And I'm no prude, but the book is laced with needless profanity. For instance, is there really a good reason to use the phrase "DeGeneris attended fucking DeLaSalle High School"? (Which, for the record, I did not.) Mr. Pittman admits he used cursing throughout the book to try to make it "edgier," since my life wasn't filled with enough scandal. (Note: This is the same reason he gave for the abundance of profanity in his children's book, *Happy Birthday, Mr. Otter*. The book was deemed inappropriate for children and never published.)

Also, I was never a member of the Doobie Brothers.

So, there you have it. While it is certainly entertaining, just know 90 percent of it is inaccurate, misleading, or simply made up. Mr. Pittman admitted as much to me, but defended himself by saying that he didn't feel well during much of the writing of the book, so he couldn't do as much research as he would've liked, and may have overdone it on the cold medicine.

Happy reading.

JON CHATTMAN is an author, writer, marketing expert, entrepreneur, and self-professed Star Wars nerd. He takes pride in the fact his two sons often hum "The Imperial March" after bath time, often in Darth Vader towel robes. His newborn, Lila, will soon learn the ways of Leia.

Foreword to Chewbacca's *I, Wookiee: A Memoir*

By "Joe Weaver," character actor

S CENE STEALERS. They come in all shapes and sizes.

Jonathan Lipnicki walked away with *Jerry Maguire* with his "human head weighs eight pounds" line. Vivian Vance nearly upstaged Lucille Ball in many episodes of the classic *I Love Lucy*. Similarly, Johns Goodman and Turturro chewed up the screen in *The Big Lebowski*. (Actually, most supporting characters shone in that Coen Brothers classic, though no one really quotes Steve Buscemi's poor schlub Donny much, but I digress.) Anyway, there are tons of examples I could list (props to the Ropers in *Three's Company* and Pat Morita in *Honeymoon in Vegas*), but there's truly only one scene-stealer who tops them all, and that's a seven-foot-five-inch furry alien in a space drama.

Yes, let's face it. No actor has stolen more scenes than Star Wars' Chewbacca—no mean feat for an actor whose lines aren't in English. "Let the Wookiee win?" He did. They did. We all did.

But there's more to this Wookiee than just a growl, an abundance of fur, and the best comedic timing this world has seen since Art Carney did Ed Norton. On screen, Chewbacca was a trusty sidekick, relentless warrior, and friend to all (just ask C-3PO, whom he carried in a JanSport backpack). Offscreen was a different story. A story that has never been fully told—until now.

I, Wookiee is an exploration of self so much deeper than space. Chewbacca's life story has taken more twists and turns than an X-wing (with far less plot holes than a George Lucas prequel). In a no-holds-barred look back at his life, the Wookiee discusses his highest highs and his lowest lows, and the Hoth snowball–sized obstacles that got in his way. Candid as ever, the star shares intimate stories of love affairs gone wrong, onset hijinks (there's a great bit that I won't spoil here involving Yoda and a bar of soap), and his offscreen struggles with a near-lethal mix of cocaine and Ovaltine.

I'm honored to lead you into this book, but you must be wondering, why Joe Weaver? Isn't that the guy from *Pete's Gas* and *Beyond the Cookie Sheet III*? (Guilty!) Why is a bit-character actor writing a foreword to a book by a big movie star?

The answer, like the Wookiee himself, is somewhat fuzzy. But it's rather clear to those who knew us in the 1980s. Chewbacca and I were the best of friends and the greatest of lovers for many years. He was and is the love of my life.

Chewbacca and I met on the set of *Star Wars: A New Hope* in its infamous Cantina scene. I was an extra, and he was, of course, a budding film star. We barely spoke then. I was just some young kid in a silly mask with plastic spikes sticking through both sides of my mouth and a wig right out of the Jim Henson factory, holding a wine glass. We talked once or twice at craft services—probably about the Lakers or something. That was it. When it was over, I collected my small paycheck, and we went our separate ways. I appeared as an extra, then an actor, in several other films. Chewbacca, as you know, went on to great stardom with the franchise.

Years later, our paths would cross again, and our lives would forever change.

One night at Studio 54, I waited in an endless line with two buddies of mine. We watched countless superstars let in with open arms: Liz Taylor, Liza Minnelli, Andy Warhol, David Bowie, and Elton John—to name a few. The bouncers were ruthless, though. They wouldn't let anyone "unworthy" in, especially not a trio dressed to the nines in JCPenney apparel. I remember one bouncer vividly. He looked like a fat Dick Van Patten. He rarely spoke, and when he did, it was to tell you to "move along." The dude wouldn't even let Halston in until Rick James gave him a heads-up who he was.

My friends and I were ready to give up and head home when, out of the blue, a gigantic, furry friend tapped us on the shoulder. "Hey, you guys looking to party?" he asked. (Or something to that effect. Over the years, so many people have asked me, "How do you understand what he's saying?" The answer is simple. Half the time, I don't. He's learned some English, but not much. His eyes, however, tell the story; they take you places the English language simply cannot.)

"Hell yeah," I said. Obviously, the big guy didn't recognize me.

"Cool JCPenney digs, brother," he said to me before guiding us toward the red rope. As we approached, along with supermodel Lauren Hutton and actor Nien Nunb (who would go on to star in a few Star Wars films of his own), Chewbacca went up to the bouncer and laid out a soft growl. The pair immediately began laughing, and the bouncer motioned all of us to come over. We were instantly let in, and from there, we partied to the wee hours.

Studio 54 was everything I thought it'd be: flashing lights, stars, dancing, glitz, glamour, and, of course, drugs all over the place. As a matter of fact, I remember seeing Admiral Ackbar do a line of coke off Pia Zadora's armpit like it was yesterday.

That evening, Chewie and I formed a bond. As you'll find out in this book, he confided in me about how he wanted to branch out beyond film and try his hand at theater. He had even been entertaining an offer to play an undetermined role in a revival of *The Music Man*, and was in the running with Sir John Gielgud for a starring role in *King Lear* on Broadway. Sadly, he was already locked in to film the Star Wars sequel (originally titled *More Adventures from Space* and later retitled *The Empire Strikes Back*). He was dismayed he probably had to put his stage dreams on hold. We shared a lot that night.

I thought that crazy night would be the last time I saw him. But following the filming of *Return of the Jedi*, Chewbacca reached out to me randomly and asked to meet for a cup of coffee. He shared more and more about his exhaustion in the business (a lot of this is recounted in these pages). The coffee chats became a regular thing, along with late-night calls. We'd often watch the same movie together from distant countries while on the phone together, much like Billy Crystal and Meg Ryan did in *When Harry Met Sally*. Following a grueling press junket for *Jedi*, Chewie asked me to go with him to his native planet of Kashyyyk. That's how close we had become. I remember his words vividly: "I'm burnt, my brother. This Star Wars thing is just too much." Tears in his eyes, he confessed, "I haven't truly been the same since the holiday special."

Shortly after *Jedi* hit theaters, he and I went to meet his family, including his supportive parents, whom I (being unable to pronounce their real names) lovingly referred to as Karen and Doug. At home, he was a hero, but he was still treated normally. Everyone looked like him. He was at peace there. He could perform where he wanted, and go where he wanted without being stopped every five seconds for a picture or autograph. Something in him was finally able to relax. Chewbacca, a Wookiee warrior who fought in the Clone Wars, and became a movie star, had simply had enough of Hollywood and wanted to make love, not war. He wanted to settle down and simply just be.

For six years, the big lug and I carried on a love affair for the ages on his home base. We were star-crossed lovers. As we came from different planets, few people (or Wookiees) understood our love. It was very difficult on him, and certainly for me; I encouraged him to channel his frustrations into an autobiography or at least a journal, which he began writing in religiously. (Many of those countless pages on legal paper became an early draft of this very book.)

Eventually, his desire to return to acting led to the end of our days on Kashyyyk, and the end of our relationship. We've rarely spoken since. So, admittedly, I was shocked when Chewbacca reached out to me so many years later to write this foreword. He'd rediscovered the aging legal pads in his old JanSport (the very one he'd used to carry that annoying droid in) in the back of his closet and had been inspired to put those memories into a book.

Initially, I hesitated to agree. I still have Wookiee scars—some figurative, and some literal. (He's a very restless sleeper, and he's strong, and well, some nights, I was physically injured as I lay next to him . . . I digress.)

"Joe, this memoir wouldn't have been written if it weren't for you," he said. After a lot of reflection, I get it. While I physically may not have him, I get him. Despite the language barrier, I've always understood him on a deeper level, and after reading the manuscript for this book, I was sold and you will be, too.

I'm not sure I could completely open myself up the way Chewie has in this memoir. You will marvel at his wordplay as I did his fore-play. In the pages that follow, our hero bares his soul and takes you underneath the fur, so to speak. He takes us on a journey from a young Wookiee growing up in South Central Kashyyyk. He recounts his early days being bullied by larger Wookiees because he aspired to be a ballroom dancer. He chronicles his formative years in high school, appearing in countless productions of Broadway hits like *Oklahoma!* and *Twelve Angry Men,* and ultimately his rise to fame in the biggest franchise in film history. And, this Wookiee doesn't hold back about the seductions of Hollywood. He opens up about drug use and spats with his costars, Hollywood romances—especially the ones that ended badly (RIP Zsa Zsa Gabor)—and riffs a bit on George Lucas himself (they didn't talk for two years because of the inclusion of Jar Jar Binks in the prequels). He also finally confirms the rumors that he was indeed passed over for the lead role in *Harry and the Hendersons.*

But, this book isn't just about hits, misses, and regrets. It's a story of triumph. Chewbacca fought his demons, overcoming drug addiction and depression, and eventually came to terms with the pressures of fame—even finally embracing the convention and Comic-Con circuit (though he's not big on "selfie" requests). And spoiler alert: Chewbacca is now a beloved dad, who has settled down and married a great woman from his planet whom I call Dolores (because I can't pronounce her name, either). They have two amazing children whom I lovingly call Bob and Mary (yep, also not sure of their real names).

This book is about dreams fulfilled. This is not about letting the Wookiee win, it's about how the Wookiee won. It's my honor to lead you readers into one of the best stories ever told—a story of a furry friend from another planet who always stood tall no matter how many proverbial Death Stars got in his way.

2

Politics, Religion, and Social Commentary

IN GOD, WE COVFEFE

YOU REMEMBER the good old days of Facebook? You know, when people said they wouldn't sign up because they didn't care what their friend's mom had for breakfast or who their high school girlfriend was dating now—that sort of thing? Well, those days are long gone. This chapter has some deep thoughts (in a very non–Jack Handey way) on topics that have probably made you unfollow half your online "friends" by now. Sure, this book is all "fake news" (a term that will endure as long as my college loans), but the themes are real and resonant and reflect the society we live in. For example, you'll get a glimpse of the obnoxious lingo today's tweens use with a Bible written just for them. You'll question why we do what we do when we shouldn't do so many things. There's a story about whether or not God exists, and we get political with a take on the GOP and truth in the Trump era. To put it mildly, this chapter has enough topical stuff going on to fill a Stefon dance party.

J. AARON SANDERS is the author of the award-winning novel *Speakers of the Dead: A Walt Whitman Mystery*. His work has appeared in *Literary Hub*, *Carolina Quarterly*, *Gulf Coast*, *Quarterly West*, and *Beloit Fiction Journal*, among many others. He lives with his girlfriend in Hollywood, where he is working on his second novel.

Foreword to Newt Gingrich's *Post-structuralism for Republicans: TrumpTruth and How to Make It*

By "Betsy DeVos,"
US secretary of education

I MUST CONFESS. All those years ago sitting in English 2155 at Calvin College and being forced to read critical theory seemed like a colossal waste of time.

I remember my professor in his hipster cords and flannel shirt and Stan Smith Adidas pacing back and forth with a piece of broken chalk in his left hand, preaching about how narrative descends into nothing but more narrative, and how information as we know it ultimately adds up to bupkis.

I didn't take it seriously then. To me—and many others, I would come to learn—post-structuralism felt like a cruel punch line to the ironic setups of postmodernism. There is no "center" anymore. There is no meaning. We're all wrong, and what's worse, we can't comprehend the wrongness of our wrong. Like I said, a cruel punch line.

No wonder academia is a sinking ship. A bunch of overeducated, tea-drinking so-called intellectuals who are more interested in navel-gazing and catastrophizing than helping our young people find jobs. (If I have to read another "poor me" narrative in the *Chronicle of Higher Education* then I'm just going to have to cancel my subscription.) But that's the lesson, isn't it? The world often changes in ways we simply can't anticipate. Like the way Donald Trump confiscated post-structuralism from liberals. That's one thing Gingrich's book clearly demonstrates.

In the fascinating *Post-structuralism for Republicans: TrumpTruth and How to Make It*, Newt Gingrich demonstrates how the election of Donald J. Trump turned post-structuralism, a liberal's masturbatory fantasy, into a powerful lesson on how to create truth.

How did Trump do it? According to Gingrich, "Trump inserted himself as the center of a forgotten system of meaning, or structure. He lifted his motto 'Make America Great Again' right from the framed cross-stitches of forgotten Middle America and made it gospel." Gingrich goes on: "These are the same folks, mind you, that have taken out loans to sit in classrooms where college professors do little more than tell them how much they don't know about the world. Of course they're angry. Who wouldn't be?"

The irony, of course, is that Trump's rhetorical move capitalizes on one of the core principles of post-structuralism: namely, that there is no natural center to anything. Jacques Derrida, a Frenchie whom you've never heard of (if you're lucky), put it this way in *Writing and Difference*:

> Henceforth, it was necessary to begin thinking that there was no center, that the center could not be thought in the form of a present-being, that the center had no natural site, that it was not a fixed locus but a func-tion, a sort of nonlocus in which an infinite number of sign-substitutions came into play.*

So there is no "natural" center, which means that centers are artificial and malleable. Infinite play! Infinite meaning! How grand!

Academics and theoreticians are so very proud of this. They love to swing their post-structural bats over the heads of the philistines

---

*Jacques Derrida, "Structure, Sign and Play in the Discourse of the Human Sci-ences," in *Writing and Difference*, trans. Alan Bass (Chicago: University of Chicago Press, 1978), 280.

around them. After all, there's a certain pleasure in telling people that their centers don't exist, then retreating to their book-infested offices and not answering when students knock on the door.

Enter Donald J. Trump. Say what you want about him, but—as Gingrich writes—he is a post-structural force that nobody has figured out how to contain. He saw the United States as a structure emptied of its meaning, and he inserted himself as an alternative center. Every tweet creates a narrative Gingrich calls "TrumpTruth," and anything that does not fit into TrumpTruth becomes "#fakenews."

But *Post-structuralism for Republicans* is about more than just Trump. It's a handbook for how Republicans can continue to take back their country. For example, in his chapter "Apostates of the Human Race: Who Needs 'Em," Gingrich discusses the theories of Steven Pinker, Noam Chomsky, and Judith Butler, treating each theory with a seriousness that frankly none of them deserve, and ultimately laying them bare as they are.

In "Teachers: Overpaid and Underworked," Gingrich calculates the shockingly high hourly wage of the nation's kindergarten teachers. As secretary of education, I will be looking for ways to bring these salaries more in line with similar professions—like, say, that of Lyft drivers.

And while I'm naming favorite chapters, "Natural Selection and Medicare: Let Them Die Already" and "In Defense of Fear: Rethinking Nuclear War as a Blessing" had me cheering in my study.

I'm still somewhat shocked that I have lived to see the day when post-structuralism turned on its creators. I now wish I had taken English 2155 more seriously, if only to better savor how Trump has beat down liberals with it.

But don't take my word for it. Turn this page and get your pens ready: We're here, we're Trump, get used to it!

A very special thanks to Pat Buchanan, my resident Derrida specialist and good friend.

MICHAEL CERVERIS was raised in West Virginia and educated at Yale and has been baffled ever since. A two-time Tony Award–winning stage and screen actor, he has toured the United States and United Kingdom with the Bob Mould Band and nowadays leads his Americana band Loose Cattle in search of green pastures and sliding-scale bar tabs.

Foreword to *It Seemed like a Good Idea at the Time: A Tedious Brief History of Compassion in the GOP, or The Chickens Have Come Home to Roost, and We Are Frying Them*, by unnamed sources within the White House

By Michael Cerveris

I UNDERSTAND THE AUTHORS, whoever they are, initially balked when their publisher, NRA Books, suggested me to write the foreword for this hastily compiled work, which they were quietly rushing to publication before the Congressional Budget Office had a chance to read it over. The writer/leakers were, apparently, put off when they learned of my inclusion on the National Registry of Elitist New York Entertainers. However, once they saw my performance in the Broadway musical *Fun Home* (at James Comey's daughter's suggestion), and realized they don't find me all that entertaining—or that much of a celebrity—they thought I'd do just fine.

It Seemed like a Good Idea at the Time will take you on a jaunty ride beginning in the dark days of the party of Lincoln, when concern for the humanity of a race of humans who had hitherto been considered property tore the nation asunder. Readers may want to treat the middle chapters like a politician in the flyover states (dropping in only when absolutely necessary) for scant coverage of unimportant moments like Hoover and his party being called to account for the Great Depression, and for a number of less great depressions suffered by many in

the decades since. Chapter twelve, "A Crook in the White House . . .
Imagine!" is a jolly fantasy sequence set in the Watergate era wondering what life would have been like in America if impeachment had
never been invented. But the book really picks up steam in the later
chapters as it follows the GOP through the salad days of the first Actor
President (whose jaunty hairstyle, affinity for pancake makeup, and
mental decline while in office prefigured the party's ultimate tangerine-
hued Beloved Ruler). What follows is a white-knuckled slalom down
the slippery slope from the Tea Party to the ruling party—all without
ever having to form a governing strategy.

Thrilling "You Are There!" moments in the book's closing chapters include a celebratory look behind closed doors at secret sessions
to draw up a Senate health care bill that even those writing it won't
read, whimsical coverage of the non-union casting call that discovered a community theater understudy from the Alaskan governor's
office and made her a star for nearly fifteen minutes, and a breathless
description of just how Dr. Seuss's Yertle the Turtle was painstakingly
groomed to lay the foundations for the party of obstruction (and one
day become Senate majority leader). A brief comic interlude explaining that Gerry Mandering is not actually the name of a senator from
North Carolina will surely be posted and shared across thousands of
social media accounts. However, triggerable readers are advised that
a last-minute coda added just before publication may cause some
distress as it attempts to put a RomCom spin on the old He Did/
She Didn't story of a doughy boy who couldn't hold his liquor in
school growing into a redfaced doughy manboy who can't hold his
temper in Senate hearings. It is less credible than presumably hoped
and certainly should not have been confirmed by the editors. But
hey, it's time we all seek unity, so the happy reader who only reads
forward and never flips back for a second look will be richly rewarded
(did someone say Cabinet position?)

I found myself desperate but unable to put this book down
(kudos here to the marketing department's paradigm-shifting use
of Super[pac] Glue on the dust jacket). You're about to find out

the answers to questions you never wanted to ask, such as, just how many White House advisers can you throw under one bus? You'll also learn just how easily inconvenient things like "the higher good" and "personal ethics" can be discarded when you just want to give the appearance of doing something. Here at last we have a book that simultaneously condescends and panders to us readers. It will be welcomed with open arms, closed minds, and, perhaps, a lack of comprehension by many readers whose educations were underfunded over the decades by the authors themselves. For that reason, the appendix filled with colorful cartoon pages will be quite handy. If you're an adult reading at a fifth-grade level or planning the syllabus for a Christian community college, this book will give you the warm, fuzzy feeling that Ozzie and Harriet were real, just as you've always believed. And if you happen to be Russian, why, it'll almost feel like you wrote it yourself. Or with your bot. As much as I enjoyed this mirthless laugh fest, I think I'm looking forward even more to a future time when I can reread this and say, "Phew, thank goodness that's behind us all."

GREGORY JBARA (@gregoryjbara) is a Tony Award–winning actor of stage, film, and television whose credits include *Blue Bloods* on CBS and *Billy Elliot* on Broadway.

Foreword to Vicki Mulholland's *Is Big Pharma "Big Brother"?*

By Gregory Jbara

WHEN A FELLOW Hollywood parent from our kids' old charter school reached out about contributing a foreword to their upcoming book, I was expecting something related to the California SB277 vaccine law or similar. Imagine my surprise (dummy me) when I realized what she *wanted* was for me to talk about the profound influence my older sibling had on my formative years! I mean, it's right there in the title! I didn't even *have* to read the book.

Truth be told, I *didn't* read the book. (There are no color pictures. Coffee table books are more my speed.) Actually, Vicki seemed weirdly relieved to hear I hadn't read it. She just asked me to sign a contract saying it's okay to put my name on the front cover. Hello, why write a foreword if your name won't be on the cover of a real printed book!? I assume the book isn't going to be very controversial, so . . . do what you gotta do, Vicki!

Anyway. Throughout my life, I have had many big talks with my big brother regarding relationships, kindness, integrity, heartbreak, and even fiscal responsibility. But if I were to list the single most profound advice he has ever imparted, I would have to say my lifelong (and, coincidentally, antibiotic-free) health is in no small part thanks to his teaching me the proper way to sanitize a public toilet.

By committing these three simple steps to my daily routine, my big brother gave me peace of mind that no porcelain bowl or porta-potty devoid a box of sanitary seat covers would ever stand in the way of a charley horse–free sit-down with the sports page.

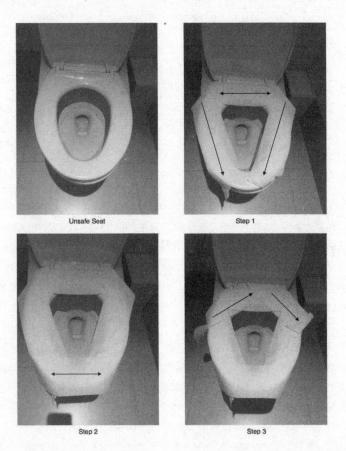

Step 1. Extract approximately 36″ of toilet paper. Lay the center atop the back of the seat and fold down both sides to make an upside-down U.

Step 2. Extract approximately 12″ of toilet paper and lay atop the front of the seat, making sure to cover any exposed bowl or seat.

Step 3. Extract approximately 24″ of toilet paper and lay in an upside-down V, covering the two teeny exposed areas on the inside corners as well as the seat hinge in back.

Before sitting down, be sure to tuck shirttails under T-shirts and hold waistbands below knees away from bowl fronts. If the toilet is armed with a motion sensor auto flush, drape an appropriate length of toilet paper over the sensor before beginning step one. Armed with this bug-blocking technique, the only affliction I have had to deal with is the occasional giggle-inducing case of tingly blue toes. Thanks, "Big Brother!"

Oh, and enjoy Vicki's book, everyone. Whatever it's about.

JOHN OATES (@johnoates), quite simply, is John Oates—a Rock and Roll Hall of Famer, author, road warrior, and formerly mustachioed icon.

Foreword to *Blank Pages: An Anthology*

By John Oates

B Y NOW, there are few people in the world who haven't heard of the mysterious book that has appeared, without explanation, to at least one person on every continent. There have been critics who have denounced our reports as a hoax; as I am one of the first to have found the book, I am here to tell you it is as real as you and I. As the finders' stories in this collection will attest, the moment it appears, life changes in an instant.

I found the book on my doorstep quite unexpectedly. There was a note pinned to the cover that said, "For You . . . For Everyone." No title, no author's name.

I examined the worn, distressed leather cover; it could have easily been a clever recreation designed to resemble an ancient tome. I turned it over in my hands and experienced an eerie sense that something profound was about to unfold. Intrigued, I carefully opened it to the first page. The paper appeared to be similar to translucent vellum. It felt fragile and smelled musty.

There, centered on the page, about two-thirds down was one word. It was written in an indecipherable arcane script that appeared to be floating above the paper. I wondered, *Is this the author's name or the title?* Looking closer, I thought the word might be from some ancient Middle Eastern language.

In the seconds it took for my mind to process what my eyes were seeing, I blinked. As if by magic, the word changed. The only similarity was the astonishing, shimmering, three-dimensional quality of the letters . . . still incomprehensible to me but now totally different from the word that had first appeared. I was drawn to the calligraphy that, although still unrecognizable, undoubtedly flowed from an artistic hand. I blinked once more and again the word changed. Now, even with my limited knowledge of orthography, I instantly recognized the bold, graphic strokes of an Asian script.

My hands were shaking as I closed the tattered cover. I took a deep breath and carefully opened it again to the cryptic title page.

What appeared before my eyes caused me to gasp for breath. There, floating above the page in black gothic-style letters was the word "God." Was this the Torah, the Koran, the Dhammapada, or the Bible?

Now, beyond intrigued, I quickly turned to whatever lay beyond the enigmatic title page. What could possibly be contained within that had not already been written, shared, analyzed, interpreted, and codified during the last few thousand years of human history?

The first page was blank . . . and the second and the third . . . the more pages I turned . . . the more blank pages appeared. Then it struck me . . . devoid of message and dogma, the empty pages were perfect and flawless. The denouement was at once personal and universal. No beginning and no end . . . for me . . . for anyone.

The stories that follow share similar stories of the book's appearances and its impact on people around the world. It is our hope that, even if you never see it, its mysteries will change you as it has changed us.

Who can say to whom it will appear next?

Foreword to Stephen Hawking's *Why We Keep Making the Same Mistakes*

By Moby

W E LIVE IN AN AGE, or an epoch, of endless hyperbole and promotion but, having read *Why We Keep Making the Same Mistakes*, I can safely and without hyperbole state that this might be the most important book ever written. I'm honored Stephen Hawking asked me to write the foreword, having long admired old rave anthems of mine.

The premise is simple: For millennia upon millennia our ancestors battled problems that were almost invariably out of their control—hunger, bad teeth, hungry bears, droughts, fires, and so forth. But somehow over the last few hundred years, humans have figured out how to gain the upper hand over most of the things that used to kill us and make us miserable. We figured out how to create enough food for everyone on the planet, we invented dentistry, we learned how to stay away from hungry bears, and we figured out how to bring water to dry and burning places. Simply put, we won.

Our old hardships were defeated, and we entered the nineteenth and twentieth centuries victorious, like glowing champions returning from a long war. We had peace, we had prosperity, and suddenly we had the ability to shape our destinies, rather than having our destinies shaped by our adversity.

And what have we done with the peace? Bafflingly, we've created sui generis hardships that put our old hardships to shame. We've invented modern warfare, an industrialized animal agriculture, body- and soul-destroying work, and global systems that create quotidian horrors for almost every person on the planet. Thus, this book.

In it, Hawking examines a seemingly imponderable question. Why, when given an ostensible tabula rasa of peace and prosperity, did we create horror?

The true kick in the teeth is that we know better, and we've done this to ourselves.

When confronted with peace, we created war.

When given adequate food, we created famine.

When given a healthy ecosystem, we created environmental apocalypse.

When given innocent animals, we created suffering.

And on. And on.

And the exasperated premise of the book is this: We're not stupid, so what the hell are we doing?

The evidence is all in front of us: obesity, cancer, heart disease, depression, and anxiety . . . rising gun violence . . . a hundred billion animals killed by humans every year . . . a climate that is increasingly incapable of sustaining human life. And on. And on. And on.

There are, simply, not very many problems we're facing that we haven't created. The book ends optimistically, with a wake-up call, asking us to look at the evidence and exert control over the horrors we create and sustain on a daily basis. But at the same time, it ends ominously, reminding us that we have a choice: reject the status quo we've created, or simply perish.

ANN MAHONEY is an actress whose credits have included *The Walking Dead* (as Olivia), *Sun Records, Bad Moms,* and *99 Homes.*

Foreword to Camila Camarena's
A Land Without Mirrors

By Ann Mahoney

"WHAT SHE FELT ABOUT HERSELF came not from adornment, not from features. Rather, it came from the strength of her maternal ancestors passed down from the source, the innate power of a woman: unquantified, unmeasured, worthy of love just because she existed."

I first read these words from Camila Camarena's heavily auto-biographical novel while in the midst of yet another audition for the "frumpy best friend," in yet another Hollywood pilot, and my mind exploded with questions—and with possibility. How could what I was longing for be phrased so perfectly by the words of this author? How did she know what I was longing for so precisely, given the vast difference in our cultural upbringings?

When I got the call from my publicist that Camila Camarena wanted me to write the foreword to her first novel, I was initially mystified until I learned the power of the podcast. I had never heard of Camila, and she had only recently discovered me. But somehow, my little homegrown podcast, *Eye of the Beholder,* had made its way to the ears of the ninety-seven-year-old matriarch of a secluded village in the mountains of Galicia. She had spent many years mastering the English language by reading battered copies of the works of Mary Shelley that someone had brought to the village long ago. At nearly a century old, Camila was determined to write her first book, and she wanted to write in English, rather than her mother tongue, to reach as many readers as possible and because, as she told me, "Your culture is so in need." As I was someone who had experienced the superficiality and misogyny of contemporary American society firsthand, she thought I would be the best person to write the foreword. Indeed, she didn't really ask me. She said simply, "You will write the foreword, OK?"

I traveled to meet her. In speaking with Camila, sitting around a fire outside her modest thatched-roof home, I felt strangely like I had come home to a place I lost long ago. Camila writes of what she knows. Growing up in that secluded village in northern Spain, she is a direct descendant of the woman who founded her village hundreds of years ago.

Camila is the mother of four girls. As of this writing, Camila's surviving daughters range in age from sixty-three to seventy-seven. She shared with me that the book was essentially inspired by her youngest daughter, Alazne. "Her birth was difficult, I was bleeding more than with any of the others, and when she was born, it seemed she wasn't breathing. Then, a wind blew into the house, from nowhere, dust swirled around, and when it cleared . . . she cried out. I named her Alazne because it means 'miracle.'" In telling this tale, Camila's eyes still welled up with tears of amazement. Her more stoic eldest daughter, Emperatriz, nodded. Camila's eldest recalls the day Alazne was born as well, but she carries with her a bitterness about her baby sister's leaving the village and their beloved mother. Alazne left the village at age eighteen to pursue what she termed "*a real* life." To Alazne, "real life" was in the United States, in Miami.

The difficulty of her birth, it seems, set the path for the difficult journey of Alazne's life. Alazne did return to the village, after a failed marriage, and many miscarriages, feeling as if she had somehow disconnected herself from the power source of her village. But she was never the same. She wouldn't eat; she obsessed about her looks; she was deeply afraid of ever showing her age and getting wrinkles, and so spent hours scrubbing herself until her skin was raw. Her mother and her sisters tried to nurse her back to health, but her habits turned out to be a long-form suicide, and she died of starvation on the eve of her thirtieth birthday.

Like the people of Camila's village, the characters in *A Land Without Mirrors* practice a religion that is also the core of their social beliefs, and their society is helmed by women. The men in the village have a distinct and honored part of the social structure as well, but the women are still seen as almost goddess-like, magical, in their ability to create life, sustain life, and pass down wisdom through storytelling.

It made me wonder if the same would be true of a do-over in the history of American women. What if we could have that do-over? What if we could start from scratch and nurture the role of women in a completely different way than we have in our patriarchal society?

The book has the feeling of a story that has been carried for hundreds of years inside the soul of a wise woman from antiquity—and it very nearly has. The novel explores Camila's vision of what Alazne's life could have been if she hadn't stepped outside the shelter of their village. "I know this is not possible. And in a way, this land is a fairytale, too. I realize this. But I do wish that I could have let my littlest go into the world knowing it would care for her, rather than the indifferent world she found." That was the end of our speaking around the fire that night, and we sipped herbal tea and snuggled into blankets as I tried to blink back tears.

Throughout my life, certain books have come to me at just the right time. I read *I Know Why the Caged Bird Sings* when I was grappling with trying to understand the complexity of prejudice in my native New Orleans. I found *Siddhartha* when I began to question my Christian upbringing and wonder if there wasn't a more universal application of my beliefs. Then, I devoured the entire Milan Kundera canon during a year where I felt I had lost my voice; his words spoke for me and to me. But this is, perhaps, the timeliest book of all for me—and, I hope, for you.

As I step out of my comfort zone as an actress into the production of a show I wrote and am starring in, I feel a bit like I am trying to facilitate a do-over in the history of Hollywood's women. And what a fortuitous time to do so, when it seems the patriarchy that has ruled the silver screen since the era of silent films is crumbling from the inside out. With my longing for change, I found great inspiration in *A Land Without Mirrors*. It bolstered my courage by reminding me of the power of the goddess, of the source of my strength, and of my ancestors when we still knew what true beauty was.

MARY BIRDSONG has made a fine career for herself by acting, writing, voice-overing, and show-tuning her way to the middle (quite literally—she played Norm Macdonald's wife, Maxine, in ABC's *The Middle*). She plays Meredith in the forthcoming HBO series *Succession*, produced by Adam McKay and Will Ferrell, and she's appeared on and written for *The Daily Show with Jon Stewart*, *Reno 911!*, and *Masters of Sex*. She is currently writing *Birdsong Dreambook: An Illustrated MOMoir* and can be seen on her YouTube channel (youtube.com/marybirdsongtv) in "365 Characters in 365 Days."

Foreword to Christopher Hitchens's Champagne, Lobster, Anal Sex, and Picnics: An Unabridged Anthology of Essays, Lost and Found

By "Lady Ann Somnia, Duchess of Douchebury"

WHEN CHRISTOPHER HITCHENS' last book, *Mortality*, was published in 2012, it included seven of Hitchens's essays, which had appeared in *Vanity Fair*, as well as a chapter of unfinished "fragmentary jottings" from his last days. Readers the world over mourned the passing of the celebrated author, lecturer, atheist, and activist; we devoured those last essays thinking they would be our hero's last published words.

The world was astonished, then, when I announced the discovery of a trove of previously unpublished works, collected for the first time here in *Champagne, Lobster, Anal Sex, and Picnics*.

Nearly all these treasures resurfaced whilst I was attempting to clean the seat-cushion covers of an old sofa bed Hitch left me in his will. I had the good fortune, you see, to be born the grandniece of one Mr. P. G. Wodehouse, who, many may know, was one of Mr. Hitchens's literary idols, rivaled only by George Orwell. In Hitch's obituary (or as I like to call it, the Hitch Obitch) in the *New Yorker*, Christopher Buckley wrote that P. G. Wodehouse was "the writer Christopher [Hitchens] perhaps esteemed above all others."

I confess, I did wonder if I might be provided for in Mr. Hitchens's will with *some* small token, but I never expected something like this beautiful full-size Jennifer convertible with removable slipcover! He was most generous in bequeathing such a handsome sofa bed to me. And, of course, the brilliant scribblings it turned out to contain. Taking its name from Hitchens's list of "the four most overrated things in life," this unabridged anthology of essays is arranged into four sections, each taking its name from one of the four items. Still, to call this tome an unabridged anthology of *essays* is a bit of a misnomer. There are essays, yes, but there's so much more!

There are short plays, a slightly torn Brawny paper towel with the heading "Cool Screenplay Ideas" written on it, followed by a series of knock-knock jokes. There's Orwellian fan fiction, Post-its packed with recipes for low-fat hash brownies, cardboard cocktail coasters filled with a sort of truncated rhyming dictionary for the word "poop," even a series of previously unknown haikus written entirely on men's briefs, size extra-extra large, and so on.

In short—genius!

Before delving into what you, dear reader, can expect from each section of this book's thoughtfully arranged quartet, I feel obligated to first briefly address one burning question: Why me? Why Lady Ann Somnia?

What (if anything) qualifies the Duchess of Douchebury above all others to write this most important, breathlessly anticipated foreword? I've no idea who the other candidates were, but I do know this—once word of my selection was made public, it ruffled quite a few scholarly feathers, I can tell you that!

But I was as devoted to the great Hitchens as one can be, particularly in the early to mid aughts, despite my sex (and I don't mean sex as in gender so much as sex as in the act of having it. I was on fire that summer. Don't know *what* it was. Pheromones? Beats me.).

Anyway, despite all that glorious sexual activity, I grew increasingly annoyed by the constant complaints against Hitchens by my lady-friends (the "Hitch-Bitches," I called them). I came to his defense whenever and wherever I could—in blog posts, podcasts, makeup tutorial videos on YouTube (or as Hitch often called it, "EtTuTubé?" Ha, ha!! He was never funnier than when he was making topical puns in Latin).

When I ran out of media-based platforms, and then proceeded to run out of paper, I kept going. I even went so far as to commandeer the stalls and walls of public washrooms, armed only with a dehydrated Sharpie and a well-lubricated love of all things Hitch. (I made a brief foray into *private* bathrooms, too, but the pushback I received proved too devastating. As a result of my work in one [former] friend's private bathroom, I received not a single dinner-party invitation or game night e-vite for a full two years. I've always detested parties, but I simply *adore* hummus and wilted salad, so it was a very bleak time in my life.)

Still, I was undaunted. I would take his message to the streets! Yes! To the very people he wouldn't *dare* let himself be seen talking to. I became a full-time Hitchens apologist.

But how, you ask, did I manage to parlay that grassroots activism (a role that was little more than glorified fan-club president) into authoress of forewords?

It's quite simple, really. Upon Hitch's death, I was in full possession of the esteemed sofa bed he'd left me in his will, and as the sole owner, I now held all rights of ownership to the literary contents acquired therein. Now, add to all that the fact that Mr. Hitchens still owed my great-uncle Wodehouse the handsome sum of twenty-three dollars and thirty-eight cents, and . . .

Here I am.

Now, I've long felt that Hitch's gift of humor had been largely overshadowed by his reputation for being what the French call *l'atheiste célèbre.* (If they don't call it that, well . . . they *should.*) I'm still mourning the fact that Hitchens isn't around anymore to keep us up to speed on who is capable of humor and who is not.

To that end, one of my very first acts as a full-time Hitchens apologist was to circulate a petition demanding that Christopher Hitchens's body be exhumed, tout de suite! This would enable us to arrange for a forensic autopsy to be performed on his corpse. ("Performed" doesn't seem like quite the right word in this context, does it? At the very least, it's terribly misleading, making one feel as if one might get a free show atop the deceased's rib cage. Alas, I am a woman, so I can't think of a better word. Damn you to hell, feminine loins!) My hope was that an autopsy would confirm what I long knew in my heart to be true—that inside the testes of the great atheist scribbler was not semen, but, in fact . . . a comedic ichor—biological proof of the source of humor.

There was only one problem: I didn't personally know any forensic pathologists. Still, I was certain we'd find a good one, somehow. And if we didn't, well, how hard could it be? After all, I'd seen several reruns of the hit television series *Quincy* (starring Jack Klugman), so I was confident I could step in if need be. I owed Hitchy that much.

Sadly, Jack Klugman wasn't available, but I did manage to track down his first cousin Saul H. Klugman Jr. (Saul wasn't very nice. And his fees were absolutely absorbent! So, to those of you who donated so generously to the GoFundMe campaign to help pay for his outrageous fees, apologies for the delay but you *will* get your tote bags, I promise!!)

Actually, there was one other problem. Sadly, I hadn't realized that Hitchens had chosen to have himself cremated. Ashes to ashes, testes to dust, as the saying goes.

Nevertheless, we made sure to send a notarized copy of the autopsy report to the family of whomever it was we'd exhumed. The relatives we contacted were downright snippy about the mix-up at first, but when we explained what the cash value would be of a standard exhumation procedure and forensic analysis such as the one their dearly departed had just received FREE OF CHARGE? Well, they were singing quite a different tune then.

So imagine just how pleased I was to discover a trove of Hitchens's unknown works, and to be able to prove what a comic genius Hitchens really was, once and for all. Now, to the book of comedy gold at hand, and its four sections: champagne, lobster, anal sex, and picnics.

Champagne is for celebrating. And in this first of the book's four sections, it's no accident that there is a heavy concentration of his most celebrated works, with wit that still sparkles. For those of you who've purchased this anthology and may be fearful that Hitchens's *most-beloved* essays aren't included, fear not! In addition to the new and more obscure pieces in this book, there are also pieces which will, I'm sure, be quite familiar to any Hitchens devotee. And in this author's humble opinion, these pieces are the Dom Pérignon of HitchLit. This first section *naturally* features Hitchens staples like "Why Women Aren't Funny" (originally published in *Vanity Fair*, 2007). If Hitchens had recorded a Christmas album, this essay would definitely have made the cut!

Many women, myself included, still owe Hitchens a debt of gratitude for taking the weight of the laugh-starved world off our shoulders. All us misguided women, desperately clinging to the false idea that we could create laughter by saying words—words we thought up all by ourselves—used to feel so guilty that we weren't funny. Ashamed, even. But after reading Hitchens's essay in *Vanity Fair*, I began to see that IT WASN'T MY FAULT! I was, after all, just a woman. A woman who can't think of anything but babies. And sometimes religion.

Hold one second, please. I'll be right back.

Sorry about that. Somebody emailed me a photo of their baby, and I had to stare at it for a couple of hours. He looked like just like the baby Jesus!

What was I saying?

Was it something about babies? I love babies. Oh, right! I remember . . .

Beyond "Why Women Aren't Funny," readers will be delighted to discover that Hitchy went on to write a whole *series* of essays in the same vein, which (sadly) *VF* decided to pull from their subsequent issues.

For the very first time, readers will be treated to new classics such as "Why Latinos Are Too Lazy to Be Entrepreneurs," "Why Jews Are Bad at Sports," "Why Colored Folks Should Be Kept Out of Politics," and "Hilarious Fat Jewish Dykes." Essays like "Mother Theresa: Filthy Whore or Garden-Variety Slut?" linger in the frontal lobes, and are no less intoxicating than a sparkling wine, created from Hitchens repeatedly stomping on clusters of, not grapes, but words—the very best words money can buy! And the results will surely leave you feeling dizzy with delight, like a great night of booze-infused debauchery, with its requisite wall-hugging, followed by the spins, then extreme nausea.

In these essays, readers will glean epiphany after epiphany about gender, faith, and nationality as they relate to comedy. For example, C.H. observes that you never hear a guy brag about his girlfriend, saying, "And man, does she ever make 'em laugh!"

That was a huge eye-opener for me. Because it's so true! (*My* boyfriend is unusual in that he doesn't mind if I make him laugh—in private. But when we first dated I made the mistake of making him laugh very hard at a party in front of people and he bitch-slapped me in the car on the way home. He was totally right. Now if we're in public and I think of something funny, I just write it on a Post-it and tell him quietly after I say my prayers at night.)

Next, I hope you like lobster, because that's exactly what the second section, or the second "book within the book," is called. Some may be baffled by the meaning behind the shell, if you will, but not I! First of all, this entire section weighs twelve pounds, six ounces. And at thirty-five dollars per pound, it *better* be good! Lucky for us, it's delicious. This is where you shall dive into a hearty helping of the many *debates* to which C.H. devoted a good deal of his later years. And in addition to his "greatest debate hits" such as the tête-à-têtes with leading rabbis, theologians, and clergy of every flavor, we are gifted here with marvelously unknown debates never before published or broadcast in any medium. In fact, the only reason we have access to them is because I unearthed from the sofa bed an old VHS cassette tape labeled "Salem's Lot," and there, not two minutes in, was a whole series of impromptu debates which for some unknown reason were videotaped, possibly by Hitchens himself. These include his debating with the guy at the bodega over whether he put 2 percent or 1 percent milk in Hitch's tea, challenging a crossing guard to discuss the merits of psychoanalysis, and telling a driver in a 1993 Honda Accord next to him on the Long Island Expressway to "eat his entire asshole" during a dead-stop traffic jam. (While some have argued that this last one hardly qualifies as a debate, they can go fuck themselves.) They've all been transcribed, and will thankfully be preserved for generations to come.

The third section is pretty much just poems and sonnets about anal sex.

In "Picnics," the very last section of the Hitchensian quatrain, has been thrown a motley assortment of different bits and pieces—like the last-minute items one grabs from the fridge to toss in the picnic basket for fear they might be about to go bad. But reader! Do not skim past these Saran-wrapped word sandwiches! Whether one is a Hitchens fan or not, one cannot deny the ripple effect that his more provocative essays have had over the last several decades. And here you will find many of these offerings:

- Faster, Kissinger, Kill! Kill! A Paper Doll Workbook for Girls Ages 8–12
- From Islam to HasBeenLam to NeverWasLam
- So You're an Atheist, but You Still Wanna Use Religious Fundamentalism to Judge, Discriminate, and Oppress Non-Christians: A Beginner Atheist's How-to Guide

Thank you, dear reader, for purchasing this boo—oh, sorry. Hold on!

Okay, I'm back. Couldn't resist. Just now I had to forward a mass email to a bunch of my best gal pals. It was this awesomely sweet poem about kittens. And friendship. And how to avoid getting raped in supermarket parking lots.*

After reviewing this unparalleled collection, one has to wonder: What was it that made us listen so closely to Christopher Hitchens? As the chorus of voices increased exponentially year after year, how did he manage to *still* cut through all the white noise? Perhaps it was the woolly mammoth–sized share of alcohol that fortified Mr. Hitchens's ability to project absolute certainty in his stance on any number of subjects. Or could it be the nearly constant plume of nicotine that gave him a sort of industrial revolution smokestack air of frenetic authority?

Mostly, I believe, it was his own unshakeable sense of rightness that swayed the masses. His *certainty* that he would win helped him do just that—WIN. Again and again and again. So, readers, as you revisit the works of our hero, I hope this tome will show once and for all that Hitchens never had the renown he truly deserved.

---

*Seriously, one of the great tips in this email on how to not get raped in parking lots is to never wear your hair in a ponytail. Putting your hair in a ponytail is basically like wearing a rape handle.

MARY LAMBERT is a singer, songwriter, and spoken word artist. She collaborated with Macklemore and Ryan Lewis on the Grammy nominated "Same Love" from their album *The Heist*. Her debut book of poetry, *Shame Is an Ocean I Swim Across*, was released in 2018.

Foreword to *Wow, You're All Fucking This Up Big Time*, by God

By Mary Lambert

I N THE SUMMER OF 2017, I was hanging out with a few friends in Seattle, at a bar called Miracle—oof, I have to stop myself already. Every time I start this story, there really isn't an easy way to describe this celestial event in a way that makes sense to my everyday non-God friends. What do you say about the babe who has it all, you know? "God is perfect"? "God is responsible for Pentatonix and British children and beagles"?

In any case, that night a cosmic friendship that transcended the space-time continuum began. I was about to leave the bar because my friend Tom never shuts the fuck up about CrossFit (and if I have to hear one more time that running in a group is *soooo relaxing*, I'll throw a kettlebell into a gaggle of jacked assholes). But as I eyed the smooth toothpicks and considered their bicep-puncturing potential, an infinite sparkling cloud appeared next to me and began muttering about politics and war and paninis.

I apologize that I can't further describe what God looks like, but you should know that God is super duper hot. Just a total smoke show.

What I'm trying to say is that God is literally just gas.

As you might imagine, it's difficult to communicate with an infinite non-being, but God is really into microdosing acid right now and figured something out with gravity or mass or quantum mechanics or something. Magicians don't reveal their secrets, you know?

We exchanged email addresses and began sending ironic e-cards and talking about the basic principles of atomic structure. It was the beginning of a powerful friendship. I didn't know how misunderstood a primordial non-being could possibly feel, but our email exchanges turned into phone calls, and I began to appreciate God's unfolding identity crisis. One evening after discussing the Taylor Swift/Katy Perry feud (the Andromeda galaxy is on Tay's side—it's a "whole interstellar thing"), God sent me a text that would change the course of history: *"lololol, what if i wrote a book."*

Now, I'm sure you picked up this book thinking, "A book by God?! In this here Barnes & Noble?! God doesn't have hands, you queer mystic!" Or, "God has all the hands! *Too many hands, God!* In any case, God doesn't *write* books anymore, you hot, blasphemous witch! God already spoke to the people a long time ago and churned out a couple of timeless bestsellers!"

Well, I'm here to tell you that God is back. And God isn't a man—don't use he/him pronouns. It's reductive. God wants you to know that God is everything and all genders. God uses gender-neutral pronouns, because God is omnipresent.

Now sit down, bing bong. You're in for the ride of your life.

The first three chapters of this book explore a hyper-condensed version of all the holy books and major religions, with detailed commentary and footnotes by God for clarification. For instance, in chapter two, God illuminates First and Second Corinthians with notes like, "omg I never said that," or, "ew gross. this can stay, shrimp are fuckin weird."

Following the holy books, God blesses us with Ten Updated Commandments ("IX: Uggggggh, you guys, I *am* the earth. Stop hurting me! I am running out of Divine Neosporin™.")! Finally, the guidance we've all been looking for!

I think you'll also be touched by the vulnerable moments of this book. The later chapters reveal that even holy immortals can make mistakes: "just so u know everything i made is perfect, except paninis, florida, and anything related to trump . . . shit, I'm so sorry. Those were huge mistakes!!!! why would anyone squish a sandwich??? bad ideas all around. plz forgive me."

What a lucky generation we are to witness the second coming in book form! I do want to warn you, reader. This isn't all about cleaning feet or ripping up baguettes in cafeterias. In the final chapter, God details how we can fix the world's issues, but I want to warn you that these revelations may lead to some uncomfortable moments. Additionally, I would like to apologize that this may have been my doing, reader.

At Christmas, which is a touchy day for God (I mean, c'mon, it's God's son's birthday—you know, the son who tragically died, then rose from the dead all cuckoo bananas, then got lost at Disneyland in 1996 during the Lion King Parade?), I gifted God a kitten. Boy, was it a good gift for a lonely cutie like God! God and this kitten are *inseparable*. Unfortunately for humanity, God hates most everyone now and thinks that the world's issues will be solved if everyone is animorphed into cats.

To be totally honest, I don't disagree, reader. God is cool as fuck, and I can't wait to be a cat.

Meow meow,

Mary Lambert

Director and screenwriter **ETAN COHEN** is known for penning such films as *Idiocracy, Tropic Thunder,* and *Men in Black III.* His directorial debut, *Get Hard,* which he wrote with Jay Martel and Ian Roberts, starred Will Ferrell and Kevin Hart. Cohen also wrote and directed *Holmes and Watson,* starring Will Ferrell, John C. Reilly, and Rebecca Hall. Cohen graduated from Harvard and received the Comedy Writer of the Year Award at the 2009 Just for Laughs Comedy Festival in Montreal.

Foreword to *The New Bible for Teenz—Bible Is Goalz!* Edition, featuring TeenSpeak™ translation, by the Straight Edge E-kewl-menical Council (and God, lol)

By Etan Cohen

CONGRATULATIONS and mad props to you, teenz! What you're holding in your hand is THE BIBLE, the book that brings 1000s of years of wisdom directly to you.

Whoa, did you just say *1000 years*? That's old AF!

I know what you're thinking—I don't need the Bible, I've got hip-hop music and video games. I'm chillaxing with my homies, pumping out hot jamz. Why do I need, like, Genesis when I have Sega Genesis?

Well, you've never seen a bible like the *New Bible for Teenz—Bible Is Goalz!* Edition featuring TeenSpeak™ translation!

The people behind this new edition have spent years talking to real teenz at Liberty University to make sure this bible would speak directly to YOU in YOUR LANGUAGE!

You'll see that God is the real bae-all, end-all on social media. He's got the most followers, and He didn't need a sex tape to do it! Are you ready to Friend GOD??? 'Cuz when you follow Him, He MOS DEF follows back! The only ghosting you'll get from Him is Holy Ghosting!

That way, you'll be 100% ready when Satan tries to slide into your DMs.

How did we do it? How did we make this bible so cool?

By using TeenSpeak™ we turned the Bible into language Real-Teenz™ like you can understand!

Step one: we got rid of all that old-people talk and translated it into TeenSpeak!

No more "10 Commandments"—now it's Squad Goalz! No more "Thou Shalt not Covet thy Neighbor's Wife." What the H-e-hockey sticks is THAT?? Instead it's "Don't 🥒 Your Bro's 🍑."

Instead of that boring story of Jacob marrying Leah and then Rachel blah, blah, blah, we boil it down to its essence: "My man Jacob bagged them thots Rachel AND Leah!"

We even dumped that stuffy Song of Songs and replaced it with the video for "Anaconda."

Has the Bible "got you like" thirsty for Heaven? Keep reading!

You'll learn how Abraham was the original OG—dude was breaking his father's idols all the time! Forget Paul's letters, we've got Paul's tweets to the Corinthians, his insta pics to the Galatians. He was the original influencer! And Sodom was the original Vegas, baby!

OK, you get it. The Bible is cool as ice.

But teenz don't just want to READ. You've got questions! Which is why we've included TeenZone™ questions, where we deal with the special questions RealTeenz™ have.

Like, "Yo, given the assumption of an omniscient and benevolent God, how does one justify the existence of evil?"

And, "What up, G? You ever peep how the Noah story bears more than a striking resemblance to the flood stories so common to prebiblical religions? And shizzle?"

And, "Yo, my main man—how do y'all account for the document hypothesis without reverting to tautological intellectual backflips and apologia?"

Well, we've got all the answers, and we put it in TeenSpeak™.

TeenSpeak™ answers all of it in language you can understand:

See? We're not afraid to answer ALL your questions!

So turn off your Instagram or, IDK, your Netflix and open yourself to a new journey! Pretty soon you'll be saying the Bible is GOALZ!!

Peace out,

Etan

3

Music

OPENING ACTS TO PERFORMANCES
YOU'LL NEVER HEAR

S INCE MUSIC is often associated with being an elixir (it's scientifi-
cally proven), it comes as no surprise that some of the best books
are music books. This ever-popular category includes moving auto-
biographies about musicians, books about music history, and even
novels that center on music to advance the story, à la *High Fidelity* or
even *American Psycho* (where would we be without Patrick Bateman's
analysis of '80s pop?). I often say some of my best friends are songs.
Actually, I've never said that before, but you get it. Our next chapter
doesn't exactly take that notion to heart, but heck, it's about music,
and even I was touched with what I just wrote . . . so here we are.
Let's read about some sex, drugs, and rock and eye rolls. Here are
forewords to totally made-up books about Aerosmith's long-suffering
manager, the hardship of finding a good band name, and even a
chance encounter between Garth Brooks's alter ego and the Purple
One. Put your metal horns down and read on.

PHIL ROSENTHAL is a TV writer and producer, best known as the writer and creator of *Everybody Loves Raymond* and as the host of the food and travel show *Somebody Feed Phil.*

Foreword to Phil Rosenthal's *Who's the Boss?: My Unlikely Rise to Rock Stardom*

By "Bruce Springsteen"

I'VE BEEN DOING THIS A LONG TIME, and I'm tired. I've been on the road for forty-five years. I've played every kind of venue you can imagine, from the Stone Pony to Wembley Stadium and everything in between, night after night. I've played four-and-a-half-hour shows some nights.

When I say I have a lot of fans, I don't mean to brag; I only mean in all those nights touring I've seen a lot of people at my shows. Now, I'll tell you a story and you may not believe it. But it's true.

There's this one super fan I'd always seen. He was this middle-aged Jewish guy. He'd come to a lot of shows, got pretty good seats, and I always saw him singing along—every word. I don't know why, but there was something about this guy I liked—his energy, his face, maybe. Even in an arena, for some reason, he stood out.

It was springtime 2009 in East Rutherford at the Izod Center (or whatever they call it now) and we're on the *Working on a Dream* tour. One night, right before our set, we were fooling around backstage and Clarence picks me up, like he's done a hundred times before. But this time, he dropped me right on my face. I'll spare you the details, but it wasn't pretty.

I didn't really know what to do, but out of nowhere—maybe it was the concussion—this idea came to me. So I told the boys, "Go see if you can get that middle-aged Jewish guy in the audience."

Everyone said I was out of my mind. But I said, "Just go see."

So, they went and got this guy, and he came backstage. I didn't want to show my face because it was kind of bloody. The boys found out his name is Phil Rosenthal, and that he writes for TV or something. (Interesting, I thought, but I don't watch anything. I don't have the time!)

He's in a state of shock, but he's backstage, and when he hears the show might be canceled he seems upset. "Do you even know what I paid for those tickets?" he said. "And how long I've been waiting for this show? This is my favorite night of the year! I already bought the T-shirt! I have all Bruce's albums, all the live recordings, hell, I know all the words."

Finally, I come out, and I tell him, "Well, that's what I had in mind. Can you go on for me?"

His eyes bulged out of his head. At first all he could say was "No!" And then, "Is he bleeding? Should we call a hospital?" But, even though it took a while, I kind of talked him into it.

Phil said he could definitely lip-synch all the songs, but he was concerned everybody would be upset that it was him onstage and not me. I told him, "Maybe they will be at first, but if they see you can do it, they won't be. C'mon, man, humor me. Just practice!"

Turned out, Phil had the moves. To be honest, he had the voice, too. He wasn't much on the guitar, but we could fake that. I'd be playing backstage. I could see him going from nervous to excited. As the lights went down in the arena, Phil Rosenthal got ready for his musical debut—the night you'll read about in this exciting and inspiring book.

We didn't even dress him up. He just went out into the bright lights in his Springsteen T-shirt and a pair of jeans. And the cheering audience . . . started booing. They weren't saying *Bruuuuuuuuce.* They were booing.

I've never heard such booing in my life. They threw things. A lot of things.

But this middle-aged Jewish guy stayed onstage. We started up the band, me playing and singing from the wings, and he lip-synched the first number, "Badlands." He was kind of stiff at first. The audience was still booing. But he had loosened up a bit by the end. He sort of said, "Screw this, I'm gonna just do it." I could see just how happy he was to be with the band and living out his fantasy. And I think the audience got that vibe, too. For one man, at least, this night was a dream come true.

After that song finished, Stevie looked at him and asked, "What song you wanna do next?"

"Thunder Road," Phil said—no hesitation—and he was supposed to lip synch it, too, but instead he just started a cappella. We never even put the vocal track on. We just had Roy on the piano to accompany him after a while.

The audience had gone quiet and thoughtful. Then he did the very same thing with "10th Avenue Freeze Out." No vocal track. And, he played guitar. He never played guitar before! Granted, we made the band louder in the speakers to cover up his mistakes, but you could tell he was giving it everything he had. He was sliding on his knees and doing everything I could do. I remember saying to myself, "What the hell have I have done?"

Phil played for five hours that night, and the audience went insane. I've never publicly said this before, but ever since, whenever I've needed a night off, I've called Phil Rosenthal. It's our little secret. It's my secret, his secret, and the secret of the lucky people who get to see him when I can't go on. (It's been tough keeping it under wraps till now, but it helps that we always gave the audience tickets to another show if they swear to keep it a secret. We make the audience sign non-disclosure agreements before the show.)

Over the years, something kind of amazing happened: Phil started writing his own songs. He started playing his own music. Half the time the audience comes just to see him, and he doesn't even do any of my songs anymore. Well, maybe he'll throw in one of mine just to shake things up. Sure, Phil's lyrics shied away from my usual themes of working class struggles in favor of other issues, like getting ready for the Emmys and the stresses of pitching a Netflix show, but musically we still have a lot in common.

Beyond our musical collaboration, we've also become really good friends. We go out to dinner all the time, and sometimes I ask his advice for songs. Phil has wanted to reciprocate. It's always been a dream of mine to do some comedy writing. He's encouraged me to bounce my ideas for sitcoms off him, but I haven't had a winner yet. I'm still trying to tweak my idea for a sitcom about the Ghost of Tom Joad. Phil thinks it's a bit too depressing. Still, it's good to have that connection now. He's a good guy, that Phil. He's got an unbelievable story, and it's never really told except as legend.

We'll have to wait for Phil's whole life story. This book starts with that first night in East Rutherford: the magical night when this middle-aged "kid," now fifty-seven, got to live out his dream. Sure, it also mentions his other life as a TV writer and food and travel host. But for the most part, this book is about Phil rockin'!

You know, that middle-aged Jewish guy in the audience taught me something that night, and I'm glad he's decided to share his story for the first time. I've read my share of books about music, and I've even written a few. This is more than just another rock star's memoir. It's about something bigger than that. It's about living your dreams, taking risks, and not giving up even when you get booed by an arena full of people. Ladies and gentlemen, Phil Rosenthal.

KEITH MURRAY and **CHRIS CAIN** are the founding members of We Are Scientists, a fairly popular rock band. They've sold hundreds of thousands of records and played most of the world's major music festivals (as well as some real shit holes). They also like to go to the movies.

Foreword to Terry Liscomb's *Bitter Emotion: My Years with Aerosmith*

By "Steven Tyler and Joe Perry"

"S TEVE, how'd you like to do a mitzvah for your old pal Terry?" reads the email, and I'm thinkin', TERRY? TERRY WHO!? Cuz I've known a lot of cats in my time—a lot of toms, a WHOLE lot of kitties, and even the occasional Siamese twin—but I don't remember no TERRY, unless you count that dude Terry Bradshaw who shows football, and he SURE don't know me (not to say hi in the street or send an email, anyway—he may be a fan). But then here comes an email from Joe, and Joe says hey, let's do this thing for TERRY, and now I'm doublin' up on flummox but I'm CURIOUS, because Joe hasn't sent an email since before they parked planes in the towers, so I know this is somethin' sorta sweet.

But it ain't! It's that old garbage dump dickhead Terry Liscomb— Terry Listerine as I liked to call him, after his breath—wantin' ME AND YOURS TRULY to put the gold stamp on his memoir. And he wants Joe on the project, too, as if one bona fide rock-and-roll tank engine ain't already one too many to grace a book by Terry Le Combover.

There's nothing I wouldn't do for Terry Liscomb. Ol' "Terry Cloth" I used to call him back in our heyday because he was so warm and so comforting and it was so easy to lose yourself in his soft embrace. So, that's like a robe of terry cloth, and his name was already Terry, so it was a very easy nickname to land on. Being Aerosmith's manager for twenty-three years—twenty-three years, can you imagine that?—can't have been easy, but Terry Cloth was there for us, through it all. Through thick and thin—and let's be honest, Steven got pretty thick there for a while, from like '77 to '81. Terry always said that Steven's appetites would get him in trouble, and they did, boy oh boy, my God. But I'll let Terry cover that in exhaustive detail in the book itself.

We still keep in touch pretty regularly, me and Terry. You know, I'll send him a yearly Christmas email, or an email with a good YouTube link, or whatever, and we've gone camping in the Tetons a couple of times. So, when he asked me to help out with this foreword and to maybe get Steven on board, it was a real no-brainer.

What's that stink in the air? Kinda like a skunk porked a dead whale that washed up on the beach—THAT smell. That's the smell of a FAVOR! Do me a FAVOR, Steven! Hey, Steven, howzabout a little FAVOR? Say, Steven! Steven! Over here, Steven! I tell ya, it never gets old—cuz it was old from the start. In this business, somebody always wants somethin', and if it ain't to blow you, it's probably a favor. Personally, I prefer the former.

But somebody owed somebody somethin', and so here it is: my stamp of approval, ill-gotten, nothing gained. As I told the shadowy figure who showed up when I wouldn't answer Terry's emails, I may have to do it, but I don't have to slip it in gently. So strap in, this book is gonna get a lot less interesting in a few pages. Enjoy it while it lasts.

Where do I start? I don't remember how Terry got brought on with the band, but it was probably the label. Back then the label was always sending somebody over to spy on you, and the game was whether you could send enough counterintelligence back their way so they didn't realize how much of their marketing budget was going up your nose. In that sense, Terry was a gift. He may have had the personality of a wheelbarrow, but like a wheelbarrow, you could depend on him to haul whatever bullshit you decided to load him up with. To this day I'm sure Terry thinks I've never had a drink in my life, much less shot up on a fifty-fifty cocktail of heroin and hooker blood, because he's the kind of guy who if he sees you bonkin' his wife and you tell him you're just helping her look for her purse, he says he'll go check in the other room.

To be honest, I had forgotten that Steven had slept with Terry's wives until I read the galley of this book, but that's just the kind of guy Terry was. He wouldn't brood or hold a grudge, he would just quietly weep into the terry cloth robe that I gave him as a gift after I had thought of my nickname for him. Terry took it like a real champ, every time he walked in on a wife bucking and snorting atop Steven—"bucking and snorting," that's how Steven liked to describe them. Then he'd do all the noises through the arena's PA system, I'm remembering now that Terry's detailed it in chapters five, six, and eight to thirteen. Terry would just kinda bite his fist and grab my sleeve and go on and on about how he didn't want to let me down, how he had to get through this, for the band, for himself, for the fans, or something. And then I'd say, "Hey, Terry, where's that robe I got you? Why don't you go put on that robe for me?" And I wouldn't let up until he was wearing the robe, and then I sure felt better.

Terry loved me! It was creepy sometimes, catchin' him staring while I was having dinner or smokin' a cigarette. Of course, people are gonna crowd around the bonfire, that's just how it goes. So you get guys like Terry peering at you with shiny little eyes in the shadows when you're a bonfire. It's not jealousy or nothin' negative, though, just the rules of the jungle.

Anyway, even though I thought he was pathetic, Terry and I always got along great. He looked up to me, like a father or a big brother, where the little brother is just in AWE. With people like that, you can't do wrong in their eyes—you're a GOD! If Terry had any issues, it was with Joe, who cut a much less impressive figure than me and yours truly. It must've gotten old, dealing with Joe's sulks, and Terry was the janitor—he had to clean up all the shit.

For me, this business has always been about one simple thing that guys like Terry and Joe never seem to get: you can slow down and take it easy in heaven. Until then, I try to divide my time evenly between the four Ps: pussy, pills, popcorn, and pleasure!

Terry always knew that being a great manager for a gang of full-tilt rock-and-rollers like Aerosmith meant keeping a constant eye on us. I often found him following Steven—peeping around corners, picking locks on his hotel room doors, buying the latest surveillance equipment and secreting it into Steven's dressing room, or his bunk on the bus, or into his house, or into Terry's own bedroom. He once confided to me that he had hours and hours—"tens of thousands of hours"—of footage of Steven's "filthy, awful exploits." He would go all misty-eyed and do that fist-biting thing and say that one day he was going to write a really dishy tell-all book. And that Steven wouldn't be able to rebut any of it legally because here were the tapes, all these magnificent tapes, capturing him red-handed. But I never really knew what he was talking about. I was mainly interested in using his cameras to do the thing where I paint eyeballs on my chin and film my mouth upside down, lip-synching Aerosmith songs. At one point, I grew a pretty killer goatee that I got to look a lot like Steven's hairdo, with tiny scarves and everything.

I wonder if Terry still has all those tapes?

Another reason Terry was such a great manager was that he never forgot that I live my life for the four Ps: pepperoni pizza pie and plates (for the pizza pie).

It don't take a psychic to know what's in the rest of this book. Well, you could read it I guess, but to do that you'd need a little time and a little interest—and I've got NEITHER. Plus, I actually AM a psychic, although I'll save that for my book. I'm sure as hell not gonna elaborate about something that fascinating in TERRY'S book.

So anyway, here's what you're gonna find in this book: the "Steven's the second coming of Christ" stuff, the "goddamn did I have an interesting life on account of having strung my horse to the Aerosmith wagon train" stuff, and the "Joe and the other guys were a bunch of children" stuff. And probably an uncomfortably large helping of business bullshit that Terry finds riveting but that anybody who's not on Adderall will sleep right through.

Is that sad? I don't know, man, LIFE's sad if you take a minute to sit down with it and look it in the eye and listen to all its horrible, shitty stories. It's like when I got involved with the Free Tibet stuff back in the '80s. There were some great parties, some fine-ass women, and the Dalai Lama is one with-it dude. But then you'd hang out with these monks who had come over to plead their case and it was like, damn, guys, maybe I'll wait till I'm dead to really study up on some of this shit. YOU'RE BRINGIN' ME DOWN!

I just hope that Steven doesn't get anyone to read this book to him. When he was our manager, Terry always saw to it that Steven was "protected," as he put it, by surrounding him with folks who read at his own literacy level—that's how all us guys in the band got our jobs. Nobody on our crew could read, nor our drivers, nor much of our legal staff. Most of the gang got by with Terry as our "translator," although he largely spared Steven his services.

"Ignorance is bliss," Terry would say, "And therefore, Steven is destined to live as the most blissful man in the world." I thought that was an awfully nice thing for him to say, constantly.

So, look—if you're reading this (and I guess you are, or else having it read to you by a great guy like Terry) and you ever happen to run into Steven on the street, don't mention whatever it is you learn in the book. Tell him it's mainly about how lucky Terry was to work under his tutelage, and how Steven has a good and working ding-dong, and that Steven was like Jesus God come back to earth with a suitcase full of scarves, and things like that.

I actually do remember one story about Terry. I was comin' off stage. I'd just torn up a stadium, wagged it around in my jaws like a rottweiler with a bunny rabbit. During the last song, Joe was on the ground, scootin' around the stage on his back but still playin' his solo. And I pulled out the Angel Gabriel and started pissin' on him. I mean all over him. And he just stopped playin', man, like—STOPPED. And stopped scootin', too. But the other guys were still playin', and I was still blowin' my neck horn, and the audience was goin' fucking WILD, so we played it out, right? And I just emptied my bladder on Joe. And so the thing about Terry is that I came off stage, headed toward the dressing room, and dude just GRABBED ME—just GRABBED my jacket and got right up in my face and yelled, "What the FUCK, Steven!?" I mean, I could smell his shitty breath.

And for the first second I was fuckin' pissed, man, cuz I thought he was tryin' to give me some kinda judgment or something. But just as quick as the rage came, it rolled on, cuz I realized Terry was sayin', "What the fuck, man—that was AMAZING!"

I gave him a pat on the cheek and walked on, but like, man— THAT'S the show that finally gets him psyched? The one where I rain gold all over Joe's face? I'm just sayin' . . . Terry's a fucked-up dude. But yeah, enjoy the read. Maybe a couple decades of premium therapy paid for by yours truly's record sales have filed down the jagged edges. Dude used to be a crazy loser, but was he there? Did he see it? Yeah, I guess he did. And even an asshole could spin gold out of that straw.

CLAUDE KELLY (@claudekelly) is a multiple Grammy-nominated songwriter, singer, and music producer whose credits include Kelly Clarkson's "My Life Would Suck Without You," Miley Cyrus's "Party in the U.S.A.," and Bruno Mars's "Grenade." He has also written or cowritten songs for such artists as Michael Jackson, Whitney Houston, Britney Spears, Ariana Grande, and One Direction. He and Chuck Harmony make up the R & B duo Louis York.

Foreword to Lionel Richie's *1-28-85: The Untold Story of "We Are the World"*

By Claude Kelly

'M NOT SURE who first coined the adage "History repeats itself," but it certainly is one of the truest things I think I've ever heard.

Let me explain.

Like just about every smart person I know, I've been doing intense research of my own to (a) get to the absolute truth on everything and (b) keep up to date on pressing issues unrelated to the current US political circus. I was shocked and ashamed by just how little international news we Americans receive. As I dug for more specifics, I was most alarmed by the lack of attention being given to the current famine in East Africa. Twenty million people without access to food or clean drinking water? Why? How? No one told us! What happened to being "woke"? How did this slip by? Why aren't the news media saying more?

Quick! Think, Claude. What did we do the last time something like this happened? What can artists do? What can YOU do, Claude?

I googled. It wasn't much, but it was a start.

"Famine" . . . then "Charity" . . . then "Music" . . . then "History." A lot of weird shit comes up no matter what you search for these days. Nevertheless, the most common result was the famous "We Are the World" by supergroup United Support of Artists for Africa.

If you don't know of it, yes, you should be a little embarrassed. There's been a lot written about it, but even if you spent hours down an internet rabbit hole googling it, you wouldn't get the whole story.

It's only one of the most amazingly crafted, unapologetically positive, megamagical moments in pop music history. It raised crazy amounts of money for hunger relief in Africa. It sold over twenty million copies. It's one of my personal childhood faves.

I stumbled on one particular (and unusually well-hidden) *Rolling Stone* article about "We Are the World." Tucked midway down the Google search page, the article announced that *the* Lionel Richie was writing a personal account of his experiences writing and producing the song with Michael Jackson and Quincy Jones. I had to hear more, and I immediately began tweeting up a storm about the book, which I was sure wasn't getting the attention and anticipation that it deserved. You can understand the complete pandemonium that happened in my brain when Mr. Richie's publisher reached out to ask me to write the book's foreword.

Honestly? I have no idea why I was chosen to write this foreword (other than all the tweeting, that is). I felt humbled. I'm just as obsessed with every artist on this record as I was when I was five years old, playing this song to death on my mom's record player in NYC. From what I've been told, Mr. Richie wanted a hit writer who's been influenced by this song and the artists on it to give a "next-generation singer-songwriter's take on the power of a well-intentioned song." I was surprised Lionel Richie even knew my music, but I was definitely up for the challenge. In fact, I've worked in the very room this song was recorded in. It started as Charlie Chaplin's studio in the early 1900s. When "We Are the World" was recorded, it was called A&M Recording Studios after parent company A&M Records. Now, it is called Henson Studios, after the legendary Jim Henson. The magic is still there. There is a respect and dignity that the large, haunting room demands. There is a legacy of excellence that you have to uphold. I felt it when I was recording there, and, after reading this book, I understand it fully.

The book is titled *1-28-85*—the fateful day in Los Angeles when "We Are the World," the most historic charity single of all time, was recorded.

I mean, c'mon! Ray Charles, Cyndi Lauper, Bob Dylan, Stevie Wonder, Michael Jackson, Hall & Oates, Smokey Robinson, Bette Midler, and Bruce Springsteen (to name a few), all in one room? All that talent, all that personality, all that makeup? Don't you want to know who was in charge? Who told each star where to stand? How long did it take them to learn the song? Were there fights over specific solos? Who was high as hell? Who didn't show up? It's literally the reality show we all wanted and never got to see. Sitting down to read the manuscript, I was thrilled: I was about to get an ultimate WrestleMania-style, Super Bowl–sized glimpse into the salacious world of rock 'n' roll. Or so I thought . . .

The joke was on me. I was looking for some cutthroat '80s celebrity death match, but Lionel Richie ain't about that, never was, never will be. Turns out Lionel is equally good at writing books as he is at writing songs. He's masterful and thoughtful all the way through. We really don't celebrate the man enough.

His take on that January day is so refreshing because it's really the only take that matters. He was involved in every stage. He and MJ knew the true intention behind the lyrics, melodies, and casting. He writes about the passion and pain that fueled this record-shattering endeavor. He tactfully explores the dynamics and dramas that ensued before, during, and after the song was made.

Beneath the wonder of all that music, magic, and money is a heavy lesson on what it really means to be an artist. Every page reminds you of the sacrifice and responsibility Lionel Richie shouldered to make real change happen in the world by way of his gift.

The chapter on Bob Geldof's greeting every star as they entered with the ultimatum "Leave your ego at the door" was an eye-opening reminder to me. Amazing opportunities can be gained and lost only by one's attitude. For example, Prince (who didn't appear on "We Are the World") was widely quoted as saying he didn't want to be a part of this musical event because the song was bad. Mr. Richie sets the record straight, telling us why and how Prince was chased away from the all-night recording session. Every personal anecdote is a reminder to musicians (myself especially) that there is always a bigger purpose.

This is a masterclass on living in your purpose, taught by a master who has always lived purposefully. Leadership is tricky. You've got to be hard at times and soft at others; Lionel Richie has mastered this, too. How else could he cowrite, record, participate in, and present the biggest charity single of all time to the world with such excellence?

Truth be told, *1-28-85* requires three full reads—though you won't mind; it's a page-turner!

On your first read, just marvel at the golden years of pop royalty.

Second read, marvel at how considerate Lionel Richie's approach is to everything. He never loses sight of the real cause at hand.

Third read, marvel at how much better you're becoming as a person. Once again, you've been reminded to focus on love as you move through life.

Now, back to what I was saying earlier about how history does indeed repeat itself.

Here we are in 2019. There is a famine in Africa. Music is still our best healing agent. All we need is a singer-songwriter to write the song and create the magic moment that will raise the money and awareness. Is anyone out there capable these days, though? Who?

Oh . . . I just figured out why I was asked to write this.

I see what you did here, Mr. Richie. Touché.

I'm on it.

ALAN LIGHT is the author of many books, including *The Holy or the Broken: Leonard Cohen, Jeff Buckley and the Unlikely Ascent of "Hallelujah"* and *Let's Go Crazy: Prince and the Making of Purple Rain*. He is the coauthor of Gregg Allman's bestselling memoir *My Cross to Bear*. The former editor in chief of *Spin* and *Vibe* magazines, Alan is a frequent contributor to the *New York Times* and *Rolling Stone* and cohosts the daily music talk show *Debatable* on SiriusXM.

Foreword to Garth Brooks's *Chris Gaines at Paisley Park: The Secret Diaries*

By Alan Light

USIC WAS AT A CROSSROADS in 1999. The teen-pop takeover was in full swing—the biggest-selling albums of the year were the Backstreet Boys' *Millennium* and Britney Spears's . . . *Baby One More Time*. *NSYNC, Ricky Martin, and Christina Aguilera were also in the year's top ten, and the nightmare of Woodstock '99 crowned a new crop of rap-rock stars. Only Santana's all-star comeback *Supernatural* was able to break the adolescent death grip on the charts.

Veteran artists were confused. Billy Joel "retired" from writing pop songs. A crazed intruder attacked George Harrison at his home. And though Prince's timely anthem "1999" was everywhere, the greatest talent of his generation was struggling through a difficult phase, having changed his name to an unpronounceable symbol in protest of his recording contract, alienating fans and the music industry. That year, he tried to follow the Santana model with his album *Rave Un2 the Joy Fantastic*, for which he brought in such guest stars as Sheryl Crow, Gwen Stefani, and Chuck D, but it was a lackluster offering.

Country music supernova Garth Brooks, meanwhile, was still riding high—his last studio album, 1997's *Sevens*, once again cleared the ten-million-sales mark. But he was clearly unsure where to go next, and in 1999, he embarked on the strangest path of his career, taking on the persona of a fictional Australian rock star named Chris Gaines. He released a soul-flavored pop album, *The Life of Chris Gaines*, complete with a *Behind the Music* episode giving the character's backstory and an appearance on *Saturday Night Live* on which "Gaines" (in signature feathered wig and soul patch) was the musical guest, while Brooks hosted as himself.

It was this *SNL* appearance that set in motion one of the oddest—and, until now, most secret—moments in pop music history.

Prince apparently watched the show and was intrigued by this new musician on the scene; he grew more interested when he saw a clip of Brooks saying that Gaines "looked a little like Prince, only fatter." He extended an invitation to Chris Gaines to come work with him at Paisley Park—with, seemingly, no idea that the artist was actually Garth Brooks.

In 2017 Brooks began chronicling his own recording career through his *Anthology* series—book and CD sets revisiting his studio catalogue and his live performances. In this fascinating, slim volume (a bonus included in the Premium Deluxe edition of the Amazon-only *Anthology 5: The Outtakes* collection), he reveals for the first time the diaries he kept during the Chris Gaines and Artist Formerly Known as Prince sessions. Since I have had the rare honor of interviewing both musicians, Brooks approached me about reading through these entries and seeing if I could offer any insight into this mysterious project.

Chris Gaines at Paisley Park offers a fascinating glimpse of the interaction between two iconic artists, curious about each other's creative process, insecure about the protocol of collaboration. Brooks is obviously at something of a disadvantage—summoned to Prince's home turf, and required to stay in character. You will meet Prince and Brooks upon "Gaines's" arrival in Chanhassen, Minnesota, in October 1999, in costume and trying to maintain his accent.

Oct. 17—Before I even got to my room, I ran into Prince in the hallway. He took the lollipop out of his mouth, smirked, and said, "G'day, mate." I couldn't figure out what he was talking about, but then remembered who I was supposed to be. I stuck out my hand and said, "Hi, Prince," but he didn't even look at me—man, I guess he takes this name-change stuff seriously. I started to say "Howdy, partner," but then I worried it would blow my cover, so I settled on "Hey, big guy." I guess he thought I was making fun of his height, because he just turned on his heel and walked away. Haven't seen him again for the rest of the day.

The next morning—either as a gesture of goodwill or revenge—Prince sends a message to Brooks to meet him on the Paisley Park basketball court. Brooks was almost a foot taller than his host, and was a decent-enough athlete that he had joined several Major League Baseball teams for spring training workouts. He is surprised by what comes next:

Oct. 18—I went to the court and there were some new Nikes, still in the box and the right size, waiting for me. I figured it was going to be easy, but he started to beat my ass, so I started explaining that we don't play much basketball in Australia. I went at it harder and harder, but damn, that little guy can play hoops! He beat me two games out of three, then four out of seven. Didn't help that I'm not used to running around with this stupid wig in my eyes! All the rest of the day I was worried that my soul patch was going to fall off, but fortunately, since he changed his outfit every three hours, I had the chance to keep gluing it back on.

Later that night, Prince summons "Gaines" to his screening room.

He was watching videos of other musicians the way a football coach watches game film. He turned on a Garth Brooks video and I gulped. "Why does anyone like this stuff?" he asked. I wasn't sure how to play it, so I said, "Well . . . he works really hard on stage." Prince—or whatever the hell

I'm supposed to call him—chuckled. "Works hard? Look at the gut on this dude!" Not sure when we're going to make any music, or if I even want to at this point.

The next section of *The Secret Diaries* documents their efforts in the studio. The Nashville tradition of cowriting and pooling ideas clearly clashed with Prince's singular vision and unprecedented virtuosity:

Oct. 20—He wanted to jam, but I don't play much more than some basic acoustic guitar and piano. He was playing all these chords I've never heard before (they're sure not on any George Strait or Kiss records). And he was jumping around from drums to bass to keyboards, then running behind the mixing board—what the hell does he need me here for? And damn, does this guy EVER sleep??? He kept me up all night—I'm exhausted. Had to skip breakfast.

Still, they roughed out a song with the working title "Funky Cowboy." The words, as Brooks scrawled them, are a little hard to decipher—or maybe he was too tired to fully remember—but one line of the chorus seems to go "Saddle up and get down." They attempted a second song which they were calling "This Bar's 2 Big 4 U," but Brooks was stymied when Prince, who didn't drink, wouldn't let him make any references to beer in the lyrics.

Soon after, "Chris Gaines" took his leave of Paisley Park. He had to come up with an excuse when Prince saw that his plane was taking him to Oklahoma—something about an easier transfer to Melbourne. We are left to speculate what Prince wanted from this meeting, though he was always trying to figure out the appeal of stars in other genres (remember that "Purple Rain" started out as his attempt to write a Bob Seger–style power ballad).

Negotiations and debates over the famous Prince vault of thousands of hours of unreleased music have continued since his tragic passing in 2016, but now that the archives have slowly started to open to the public, perhaps someday we will hear the fruits of the Gaines-Glyph summit, or find out if Prince ever figured out who was under that wig.

And maybe, just maybe, Prince was slicker than Brooks's account makes it seem. Just look at an interview Prince gave to *Rolling Stone* back in 1990. "You can always renegotiate a record contract," he said. "You just go in and say, 'You know, I think my next project will be a country and western album.'"

CARLY JIBSON (@carlyjibson) is an actress of stage and screen. Her credits include *Cry-Baby* and *Hairspray* on Broadway, *One Mississippi* for Amazon, and Greg Garcia's *The Guest Book* on TBS.

Foreword to Carly Rae Jepsen's
On Call Waiting

By C-A-R-L-Y J-I-B-S-O-N

MANY EMOTIONS, thoughts, and memories flooded my mind as I eagerly ripped through the pages of Carly Rae Jepsen's *On Call Waiting*. As she eloquently recounted the events that led her to the level of superstardom we've all come to admire, I started thinking about my own time line in tandem to hers, and how serendipitously our paths have been entwined. Just like Carly, I, too, was just a "young girl who wanted nothing more than to make people smile." I felt such a connection with her drive, tenacity, and ambition to take this industry by storm. But particularly as I read chapter four, "I wrote my first album at six, in twenty minutes," it really started to dawn on me that we had more in common than just a dream . . .

You see, I've spent the last seven years of my career being confused for this lightning-rod pop star who burst into our hearts in the summer of 2012 with her addictive hit "Call Me Maybe." The song even served as the soundtrack to the Summer Olympics as the theme for the athletes as they prepped to take on the world's most difficult test of human capability. People lost their goddamn minds for this song, this singer, this artist. But no one person was more personally affected by her explosion on the scene than I, Carly Jibson.

You see, the fall of 2011 was slated to be the release of my solo album *Best of Me*, which I wrote, coarranged, produced, and performed. I worked tirelessly on those songs, as they would be my debut in a new style of music, completely unlike the musical theater I was more popularly known for after my ten-year stint in the Broadway community. After months of preparation, we launched the album on iTunes, Amazon, and CD Baby (for you millennials unfamiliar with the site, this was an outlet people used to use to buy *physical* copies of CD's. I know. Mind. Blown.).

I was so excited! What will people think? How will fans react? Will people relate to the art I've put into the world? All these questions circled in my mind as I trepidatiously threw my "baby" to the proverbial wolves.

To my surprise and complete ignorance, our fabulous Carly Rae Jepson had just *also* released her sophomore studio album, *Kiss*, earlier that week. As both records raced the waves side by side (it helps me drink less to think of it that way), I became inundated with messages, texts, phone calls, and emails. I JUST HEARD YOUR SONG ON THE RADIO! one friend from Denver messaged me. I CAN'T BELIEVE I JUST HEARD MY SISTER ON THE TOP 5 AT 9, my sister Carlee (yes, I have a fucking stepsister named Carlee—the levels of my identity crisis run real deep) boasted on her Facebook wall.

"HO-LY SHIT! Is this real?" I thought. "Have I become an overnight success? Is the album just *so* damn good that simply uploading onto iTunes has caused a frenzy in the music industry?"

Just like Carly says in chapter eight, "My dreams were all coming true," *my* dreams were all coming true! Any validation I ever needed was right in front of me. It was the most exciting moment of my entire career . . .

. . . that lasted for about twenty-four hours.

Some very simple (and humbling, might I add) research informed me that I was *not*, in fact, the artist boasting the number one single on the billboard charts. It was my long-lost "twin," who is quite literally the walking physical anthesis of me, with her long, lean structure and flowing brown locks. (You can go ahead and IMDB me now to see what I look like. Please, I need the clicks to feed my star meter.) Carly was the true victor. And look, I accepted this defeat with dignity and vodka—I mean grace, lots of grace.

But there was far more to the story than I was ever prepared for, for she was about to come stomping right onto my home turf, the Broadway stage. In the spring of 2014 she made her Broadway debut in Rodgers and Hammerstein's *Cinderella* as the heroine in a sparkling gown who has been stealing our hearts for years. "I couldn't believe it was happening; it was like a real-life fairytale," she recounts. "I was just so grateful to be there, surrounded by that caliber of talent. I was so very humbled by this experience, it was more than a dream come true."

"Damn it," I thought while reading that. I was so ready to hate her, for her to be terrible, but to my dismay, that couldn't have been farther from the truth. She was lovely, and talented, and from what I heard, kind to everyone she encountered.

For fuck's sake, is there no end to this Canadian goddess's list of awesomeness?!?!?

The answer, of course, is unequivocally no.

But I couldn't be happier for her success, for *our* success. After all, you can't imagine how many confused (and later disappointed) Twitter followers I have garnered in the mix-up. But this isn't about me, this is about Carly. I feel this book is a pivotal addition to the world of literature because it not only gives us an illustrious explanation of who Carly Rae Jepson is as an artist, but also an ironic and much-needed reminder of who Carly Jibson is not.

You're probably wondering if we ever met in person and if I ever got to tell her these hilarious and heartbreaking kismet tales. Sadly, I have not. I'm sure, to her, mine is just some weird name that pops into the search engine when she accidentally misspells her own name while trying to google herself . . . Or is that just me? Well, that is of course until she reads this little tribute I have managed to sneak into her book!

So now you're probably wondering how I came to pen this foreword. Well, the truth is, I used to date the editor of this book way back in the day, and let's just say he owed me one. OK, I begged him. OK, I blackmailed him . . . Whatever! I mean, shit, after seven years don't I deserve something? Shouldn't I have a piece of this pie?!?!

I'M CARLY JIBSON, TOO, GOD DAMN IT!!! So, please have fun reading this book! Then tell everyone you know to read this book! It would make a great Christmas gift, or birthday gift, or "congratulations for getting out of rehab" gift. Just do it. Because if one more asshole who thinks he's clever sings that goddamn song to me after I introduce myself, I am going to lose my fucking faculties and burn this place to the ground!

Enjoy!

Carly Jibson (the OG)

JOE GITTLEMAN, aka "the Bass Fiddleman," is the bass guitar player for the Mighty Mighty Bosstones.

Foreword to Ken Casey's *The Lucky Lefty: My Dropkick Journey*

By Joe Gittleman

REMEMBER THE FIRST TIME I saw Ken Casey and the Dropkick Murphys play like it was the day before three Wednesdays ago. This was the first show of the Boston on the Road tour in Decatur, Georgia, in 1997, and the Murphys were opening for my group, the Mighty Mighty Bosstones.

Well, more accurately, they were opening for the group opening for the group opening for the Bosstones. In any case, I was eager to check out this buzzworthy unit folks were calling the best band to come out of Quincy since the other band came out of Quincy. As he thumped away on his left-handed Precision bass, Casey and the lads barked out their final number—an eerily familiar three-chord cautionary tale seemingly intended to remind the two skinheads in attendance not to leave their squat without bus fare—one thing became crystal clear: this is a band destined to go on and play Raleigh tomorrow.

Now, reading the band's story through his eyes, I got lost in these pages. As the architect and founding member of the band, Casey is the one man who could truly do justice to the band's story. His graceful prose serves as a reminder that things are not always as they appear. Behind the Murphys' mayhem sits a thoughtful man, gentle and quiet, but somehow, he's always just as loud as Dropkick front man Al Barr in the mix. Here, Ken graciously lets us in to his raucous world and invites us to sit and chat a while. Have a pint. Have a laugh. Buy a T-shirt.

Ken and the Murphys made it to Raleigh back in '97, all right. And that was just the beginning. You'll find the rest of the story here, from the millions of dollars Casey and the lads raise for charity and brushes with Academy Award–winning directors to confetti cannon pranks gone awry. After a decade grinding it out in the trenches, they found their way back home to the hallowed grounds of Fenway Park. They wrote songs that made our city sing. Some say they killed "the curse" and helped the Sox win. Doubters can doubt but the fact remains, the Sox have NEVER lost a game on a day the Dropkick Murphys played Fenway.*

---

*Does not include interleague play, performances off the field, or rain-shortened games.

JOHN ONDRASIK, known by his stage name Five for Fighting, is a multiplatinum-selling singer-songwriter and record producer. His hit songs include "Superman," "100 Years," and "The Riddle."

Foreword to Hoobastank's *Terrible Band Names: A Chronology of Rock History*

By John Ondrasik and/or Five for Fighting

MARTY MCSORLEY got into three fights that afternoon. That was his job. He won them all.

It was the late '90s, and the reign of the male singer-songwriter was over. At least, that's what my record label told me. I had just finished my first album on EMI Records, the Beatles' imprint. A twenty-year slugfest of rejection, perseverance, and ego, and my audacious delusion was realized: I'd gotten the elusive record deal, and I was a priority on the label. So when the president of EMI, a legit music dude who produced Tori Amos's masterpiece *Little Earthquakes*, told me John Ondrasik (my name) wouldn't do and that I should come up with a band name, I was properly pissed off.

To clarify, there is no band. There has never been a band. It's always been little ole me and a group of wonderful (much more talented than I) hired musicians, for better or for worse.

Inspired by McSorley's bouts, I sarcastically spouted out, "OK, how about Five for Fighting!?"—my expectation being he and his staff would hate it and fold.

For those who don't know, "five for fighting" is a penalty one receives for fighting in hockey. Yes, they fight in hockey, and like all bad boys after fighting, they are sent to their "time-out room," though in their case it's the penalty box. You sit five minutes in the penalty box for your fisticuffs, ergo "five for fighting."

Marty McSorley was Wayne Gretzky's on-ice bodyguard. In the NHL, if there ever was a body to guard, it was the Great One's. Hockey is a game of skill and grace—with a large serving of intimidation. Back in the '90s, most teams had a protector, or a goon, to deter the opposition from bullying or injuring their star players. Now, some goons could actually play hockey, but most were just street brawlers on skates. McSorley was a solid NHL player, but he was loco and would fight anyone at any time. So when the LA Kings traded for Wayne, no way was he coming without Marty. They were a package deal. We were all in awe of the greatest hockey player of all time. And we adored Marty.

Still, I expected my sarcastic suggestion to meet with immediate rejection. But the president of EMI loved it. The label loved it. Everyone loved it!

They were crazy. It likely cost them over a million records in sales. Oh well. With that, FFF the "band" was born.

A name like Five for Fighting doesn't musically reflect the piano-playing crooner that I actually was. Five for Fighting sounds like a band that should be opening for Metallica or Megadeth. As a new artist, you take any gig offered to you, no matter how bad, embarrassing, or weird. So, for early gigs in my career, I would find myself booked into odd lineups with heavy metal or punk bands. Like any good newbie, I would show up with my keyboard and play my songs.

Since I was six years old, my imagination had run wild fantasizing about what a successful touring musician's life might look like. Raging, Ecstasy-laden wannabe Norsemen moshing to my ballad "Superman" was not a vision I had conjured. But it was now my reality, thanks to the name.

Most bands come up with weird and seemingly irrelevant names for themselves—with the notable exception of Hoobastank, of course, my buds who asked me to write this foreword. (You tend to like the name if you like the band.) But a lot goes into coming up with band names—usually, it takes more thought than an offhand, sarcastic remark.

As the guys of Hoobastank explore in the pages of this book, what the hell is U2 (You Too?)? Who came up with the Rolling Stones or the Beatles (clever!)?

You'll find out how a band originally called the Pendletones came to be called the Beach Boys—surprisingly, it took a lot of thought. At least Black Sabbath fit the marketing plan—way better than the Polka Tulk Blues Band did. The Who, Talking Heads, and Sex Pistols caught a wave. Queen got it right when they changed their name from Smile.

Like all things musical, names can be subjective. (Though they'll spend a whole chapter mocking it, Hootie & the Blowfish is damn memorable in my opinion.) But whatever your take, these entities are actually bands, who form, change their names a few times, break up, and then reform for their third $100 million farewell tour (sorely needed to finance their multiple families and manager lawsuits).

Look, I'm no Jeff Bezos, but I'd think for a singer-songwriter the label-marketing plan might be, oh, I don't know, let's make sure record-buying fans know the name of the songwriter who writes the songs . . . But I guess not!

Shakespeare wrote, "A rose by any other name would smell as sweet." After reading *Terrible Band Names*, I had to wonder if that's true. Would The Band by any other name play the same? What *is* in a name? Read on and find out.

4

True Crime

TAKE A BITE OUT OF IT

W E'VE ALL HEARD THE SAYING "Crime doesn't pay." Well, in one sense, that expression is total bullshit; crime novels are some of the best sellers of all time, from Truman Capote's *In Cold Blood* to Curt Gentry and Vincent Bugliosi's *Helter Skelter*. And that genre, when done right, soars in film and on television. (Heck, it even worked for pop star Richard Marx. Who could forget the mullet legend's tour de force performance as a possible murderer in chapters one and two of his hit song "Hazard"? That's right, two chapters!) Some of what you're about to read is torn from today's newspaper headlines—not literally—while others simply will disturb and intrigue you. There's even a twist on Central Perk that will haunt you forever—it's even more unsettling than the loose gym shorts episode. In a nutshell, delve into some deeply disturbing stuff even though it's all phony-baloney.

SIMEON GOODSON (@comedysim) is a comedian originally from Brooklyn currently doing stand-up in China. For more, visit Facebook.com/InSimWeTrust.

Foreword to Eric Schlosser's *I'll Be There for You: The True Story of the Central Perk Murders*

By Simeon Goodson

N O ONE TOLD ME life was going to be this way. My job was a joke, I was broke, my love life was dead on arrival. It was like I was always stuck in second gear, when it hadn't been my day, week, month, or even my year.

Little did I know how good it was.

Although the job was in a small coffee shop, it was located right in Greenwich Village. The name of the place was Central Perk. My job was to keep the place neat. I wiped down tables and swept crumbs from off the floor. I would clear and wash coffee cups after guests left. Chances are, if you came there, you probably wouldn't even have seen me. It didn't require a college degree, it allowed me the liberty to pursue a career in stand-up comedy in the evenings, and best of all, it paid cash. No taxes, no paperwork, sometimes even a few dollars in tips if we were particularly busy. Not glamorous by any means, however, to my neighbors in East New York, Brooklyn, I might as well have been working in Beverly Hills.

The place was trendy, with cushioned chairs and small tables filled with authors and doctors sipping cappuccinos. Museum staff and fashion buyers stirring raw sugar into their espressos. Lawyers and students nursing soup bowls full of Americanos over the course of an hour. All of them white. In all my time there, I'd seen only a handful of black people. Honestly, it had to be a good ten years. There was a large couch in the middle, often occupied by the same six people:

three men and three women. Two of them were brother and sister. They all seemed to be in some kind of endlessly changing configuration of living situations and (with the exception of the brother and sister) sexual relationships with one another. Although they could loosely be characterized as "friends," their relationships with one another seemed . . . antagonistic. And that's if I'm being charitable. To be honest, they were outright hostile toward one another. They were constantly ridiculing one another; barely thirty seconds seemed to go by without one of them attempting a wisecrack at someone's expense. But tensions seemed inevitable with a group that spent such an alarming amount of time together just hanging out.

My manager, Gunther, served most of the customers, handled the money, and prepared the drinks. He had a strange obsession with the friends on the couch. He would often drop whatever he was doing to accommodate them. Sometimes he would attend their private functions, like a birthday party or a bachelor party. I found it odd that he would want to befriend people who were so nasty to each other. The things they would say and do to him were things I would find dehumanizing if done to me. They would tease him about his appearance, his career, his sexuality. They would use him as a prop to make one another jealous. It was an awful way to treat someone. Although our relationship was that of employee and employer, I often tried to converse with him about this relationship he had with these people. But he would brush me off, saying something like, "That's just what friends do."

Gunther was particularly obsessed with one of the friends. The shorter blonde one, Rachel; she had actually worked at Central Perk for a few years. He lusted after her blindly, despite a complete absence of reciprocation on her part. He would attack her male suitors, berate her boyfriends, whisper their betrayals in her ear. Although she never returned his affection, she did seem to revel in it. Daily she would return to the coffee shop with her dates, loudly recounting her sexual encounters with strangers and the men in her friendship group, especially the tall, weird one, Ross. Each of these episodes tore Gunther apart, but emboldened his resolve that they would one day be together.

Of them all, Ross was the one I liked the most, or perhaps the one I disliked the least. As per my recollection, he even dated a black woman once. Rachel and Ross had a strange relationship. Apparently, he, too, had lusted for her since childhood. He, too, had sabotaged his own relationships to make room in his life for her. After a lifetime of pursuit, after a series of failed attempts to be with one another, Ross eventually convinced Rachel to reject a job in Paris so they could be together. (Unfortunately, that wouldn't last long.)

Just before she was to board a plane for Paris, Gunther also professed his love for Rachel. It is difficult to explain the horror on his face, after being rejected, when the friends casually strolled into the coffee shop the day after she was to leave the country. Gunther was humiliated, retreating to our little storage room. There, he screamed into napkins with tears flowing down his reddened face. Cups and saucers were broken, spoons and sugar packets strewn across the floor. I did my best to accommodate the guests (including the six friends on the couch). Joey, who'd briefly worked with me at the café, commented how he had never seen me before, and some asked of Gunther's whereabouts. I was short with them, perhaps even angry with them, knowing my manager was having a breakdown less than twenty feet away. I could only imagine their laughs and callous put-downs had they learned they'd broken a man so absolutely.

In hindsight, my compassion was a mistake. Had I known the ease with which Gunther would betray me, I would have exposed his embarrassing little tantrum in a heartbeat. That shift would be my last at Central Perk; the day would be the last normal day of my life.

It was the following morning when the bodies were found. Naked in bed, a single bullet in Rachel Green's head, multiple in Ross Geller's. I hadn't known their full names before this; I will never forget them moving forward.

Many of the Central Perk customers, including four of the surviving friends, reported a black man whom they'd never seen working before, who acted nervous when asked about the regular manager, Gunther. I was described as "suspicious" and "out of place." There was no paperwork to verify my claim that I had worked there for the better part of a decade. I was questioned by police as a person of interest. Everything I've written thus far is the same information I relayed to the police. Instead of accepting the information at face value, they doubled down on my guilt and tried to convince me I had committed atrocities I could never imagine having committed.

The police questioned me about the murders and also about Gunther's whereabouts. My alibi was that I was traveling around the city performing at various open mics the night prior. They claimed they were unable to corroborate any of these performances. Sign-up sheets had been thrown away, bartenders had been indifferent to my presence. I only carried cash, so I couldn't verify any of my purchases with a debit or credit card receipt. Apparently, they believed that I was responsible for the murders of Ross Geller and Rachel Green as well as the disappearance of Gunther. The media jumped on the police narrative, publishing my name and face in the paper with the damning allegations.

Months of my life and thousands of dollars in attorney fees were wasted trying to clear my name. It wasn't until Gunther turned up in a New Jersey motel with a dead prostitute wearing a blond wig that my name was cleared and I was freed. Reports said he wept the name "Rachel" while the police arrested him. The entire time, seeing my face on newspapers and television screens, and never once did he come forward to verify my claim. I had never known betrayal so deep. I won a settlement from the City of New York and moved to Colorado to start my life anew.

I would like to thank Eric Schlosser for putting the story of what happened together, and the publisher for allowing the true story to be told. At first, I found Schlosser's recounting of this ordeal a bit painful: the interrogation, the imprisonment, the mocking at the pens of the media. The events recalled in this book ruined many people's lives. Three people's flames were snuffed out permanently. There are details surrounding this case that have been outlined in this book of which even I was unaware. At the end of the day, though, what do I really know? After all, no one told me life was gonna be this way.

THOMAS LENNON is a writer and actor from Oak Park, Illinois. He has appeared in dozens of films and was a member of the influential sketch-comedy group *The State*. His novel, *Ronan Boyle and the Bridge of Riddles*, is available from Abrams Books. Lennon lives in Los Angeles with his wife, actress Jenny Robertson, and their son, Oliver.

Foreword to Vincent Bugliosi's *Sock Puppet Mozart: The Life and Gruesome Death of Randy Masterson*

By Thomas Lennon

FROM TIME TO TIME I receive requests for an interview about the great Maister Randy, as I was one of his pupils at his notorious Friends and Me Puppet Academy in the late 1990s. So when the publisher prepared to release this book about Randy's life and crimes, it turned out that I was one of the few people who had known the man himself, more than the legend—so, naturally, they asked me to write this foreword.

Friends and Me was housed deep in an abandoned borax mine on the outskirts of Searchlight, Nevada, a town composed predominantly of outskirts. After seeing the VHS footage that the Nevada State Police recovered from the mine, people have wondered if the academy was really interested in the art of puppetry—or was it just another doomsday cult, worshipping a set of satanic sock puppets that Maister Randy would force his followers to wear on their genitals as they danced around to the music of Erasure?

The truth is, it was a little bit of both. Some satanic stuff, some pretty good puppetry classes. Way too much Erasure if you're not into that stuff (which I, for one, am not). Also, there were a lot of psychotropic drugs and a fun spaghetti night on Tuesdays. Sometimes we just looked around the mine to see if we could figure out what borax was. Nobody ever did.

The Great Maister Randy was born Randall Bart Masterson in Valparaiso, Indiana, in either 1939 or 1959, depending on when you asked him and how much ayahuasca he had taken.

When he was an infant, the local pediatrician told Randy's mother, Joan, that he would live for three weeks, "best-case scenario." Endlessly outliving his own shelf life gave Randy a great joie de vivre, and it explains why he would celebrate his "death day" every twenty-one days—a practice described but not explained in this book.

Joan and Theodore, or "Tank," as Randy's father was better known, sold handmade butter churns from the trunk of their car to the Amish, Quaker, and Mennonite communities of the Midwest. The churns were shoddily made and dangerous. (The wooden handles of the churns they sold would overheat, and then catch fire and explode, leaving their operators burned, surprised, and blinded by butter.) There is also good forensic evidence to suggest that the trunk of the Mastersons' car had a major gas leak.

The Mastersons were able to sell the dangerous churns for longer than you might imagine. This was because the victims had no telephones and had to hunt the couple down using Amish technology. Eventually, Joan and Tank were chased out of the state by a polite mob wielding well-made pitchforks. Joan and Tank were never very interested in raising a child anyway, so they ditched their young son and hightailed it to Canada, leaving little orphan Randy to fend for himself in the parking lot of the Star Plaza Theatre in Merrillville. After he described this incident to me, I often wondered if this marked the beginning of Randy's complicated lifelong dedication to the performing arts.

At age five, Randy turned to a life of crime. By nine he was being held in a state of Indiana juvenile detention facility. Randy's cellmate was the Hoosier State's most famous ne'er-do-well: a tiny, sharp-eyed teenager named Charles Manson. By all accounts, Manson and Randy became fast friends. Manson taught Randy chords on the guitar and how to hide in plain sight. In exchange, Randy taught Manson how to throw his voice, a skill Randy had excelled at from birth. After their escape, subsequent capture, reescape, and recapture, both boys were released on the condition that they never return to the state of Indiana.

Manson drifted out West and tried his hand at the music scene. He never returned to Indiana. Manson's parting gift to Randy Masterson was the vague nickname "Mister Randy," which he carved deep into Randy's leg with a roofing nail— M-A-I-S-T-E-R R-A-N-D-Y—producing a typographical error that would linger forever.

Randy made it across the Illinois state line and into Cook County, City of Chicago. The famous winters there were as fierce as had been described by everyone since the beginning of time.

Now a full-grown man, Maister Randy could be spotted from blocks away as he prowled the city's Loop area. Randy did not blend in. This was likely a result of keeping his hair in a longstocking—two eight-inch braids pointed out at right angles from his head, which looked charming and assertive on their impish namesake but on a grown man was at best unsettling. Later, Randy would merge the braids into one, and send them upwards, jokingly calling himself "the Randicorn" as he frolicked down State Street, pausing only to poop in the gutter "just like a real unicorn would."

This was one of the reasons people at the time were fairly certain that Randy was addicted to glue.

It was here in the Windy City that the great Maister Randy began to take the shape of the artist I would know and love, and whose puzzling, intense journey is the subject of the following tome. I hope that reading these details about Randy's childhood, which were not included in the book, will help you to understand the man on a deeper level.

During the 1950s through the 1980s, the city of Chicago was the number one cash donor to the Irish Republican Army, a terrorist organization. Money was collected in Chicago's Irish bars for "widows and orphans in the North." This money was actually to fund the IRA agenda. A strange triangle trade began: money and weapons to Belfast—guns out onto the Northern streets—and then secondhand socks back to the city of Chicago. The socks had been thrown away by the people of Ulster and collected in a dumpster. For no apparent reason other than confusion, an old priest put the discarded socks into the empty gun boxes and mailed them to Butch McGuire's Bar on Division Street, Chicago, Illinois, U.S.A.

The old Irish socks hit the streets of Chi Town that spring. The young Maister Randy had sniffed several pints of glue when he stumbled upon them. He covered his hands and performed an extemporaneous sock-puppet show that lasted for nine days.

The rest is, as they say . . . part of an ongoing FBI investigation.

Whatever your preconceived notions about the Great Maister Randy, I hope that you can approach this new volume with fresh eyes. Try to separate the man from the hours of disturbing VHS footage that you've seen. Those tapes are only part of the story. Set aside the satanic stuff, the spaghetti nights, the sock puppets bouncing on boners, and try to see the Randy Masterson that I knew: a frightened young genius from Valparaiso, Indiana, deeply committed to his art and hopped up on glue. A man who would either change the world, or die in a shootout with the FBI in an old borax mine.

. . . or perhaps *both*.

Your friend,

Thomas Lennon
O'Hare International Airport
May 2018

STEPHEN KELLOGG (@stephen_kellogg) is a performer, songwriter, and speaker.

Foreword to Bart Haskins's *The Troubadour Murders: Homicide, Justice, and One Family's Fight to Pick Up the Pieces*

By Stephen Kellogg

EVERYTHING YOU'RE ABOUT TO READ IS LIBEL AND LIES. Obviously, I have a very different take on the story this book tells. I am the defendant; Bart Haskins, the complainant. You will read his version of events, not mine. He is wealthy and famous. I am not. He won the case against me with a unanimous jury convicting me on all counts. And yet, I tell you, as I have consistently maintained, I am innocent of the crimes outlined in this text. Memory is a liar and a thief. A sly fox with no shame in telling you things were one way when you know damn well they were another. At once the cat and the canary, memory will rob your mind of its most treasured contents without bothering to let you know you've been unburdened of the truth.

You can lie to yourself and act grateful to have lost the stories that would lay bare your bad (or worse still, uneventful) behavior. But I choose not to kid myself. Ever. It's no longer a luxury I have. I *know* that I don't know.

Someone, somewhere knows the whole truth. Hiding in some shadow, there is evidence; blood on the hands of the real culprit. But the media made a circus of my trial, as they so often do. Millions of people watched on TV as I was portrayed as a man who was unrecognizable to me—the alleged "troubadour murderer." The beast needed to eat, and they fed me to it without hesitation. An outraged public devoured me because it was the easiest thing to do—far easier than to consider the killer still at large, with motives unexplained.

Bart Haskins dug through my past and painted me into a corner of unlikability that no one could escape from. While this book explains, at length and in Haskins's voice, my circuitous road to ruin, the publisher offered me a paltry thousand words to redeem myself.

A thousand words to define a life. Where does one begin?

As I write from the cold confines of a prison cell, I'm still not sure my words belong in a book about the young men I am accused of murdering. My invitation to play this small part in the publication is a decidedly cheap form of publicity. With my contribution, I'm given to understand, many more people will read Haskins's account. In all likelihood, dear reader, you already believe I am to blame for the death of those three concertgoers on the night of November 14, 2015. I probably would believe it, too, if I were you. Nevertheless, redemption is a bugle, and I seek to be vindicated, so I'm taking this opportunity to share what I do remember.

I am (or was) a singer and songwriter. I had never met the Haskins family until the infamous night they came to my concert in Cambridge, Massachusetts. I was told that the Haskins family owned the largest investment firm in eastern Massachusetts and that they would be coming to my preshow meet-and-greet with a large group. They were excited to be introduced to me.

The group arrived late and in a state that I described to the jury as "well lubricated." They managed to fill the room with the scent that seems to ooze from the pores of the extremely wealthy: an odor redolent of vodka, steak tartare, and entitlement.

Years of bending the system to ensure one's own buttered comfort tends to make people bossy, and their family was no different, despite how Haskins describes his sons in the first chapters. They dressed in outfits curated to appear casual. They talked over everyone, including me. I remember one informing me, "You're going to come perform in my backyard." They told me which songs I was to play and laughed among themselves as they remarked, "Don't worry, we'll feed you." As though I were a stray dog.

It's true that I did not like them from the start. If I'm being honest—and I am—I found them repulsive.

We exchanged a few short words before the show. As a preemptive strike against the rudeness they exuded, I asked them to please be respectful of the performance. It is also true that later, during the concert, I called them out on whatever I heard them yelling. But as I said on the stand, I no longer trust my memory of what they said. We shouted at each other in front of 650 people that night. Me on the lip of the stage imploring them to mind their manners, and eventually abandoning my own. I said things I now regret in a way that I now regret. It wasn't a good look.

Somehow, between then and now, history conspired against me. I know that must be hard to imagine, given the overwhelming evidence found at the scene of the crime, the guitars, the original set list, and such. It was clear no one believed me when I told my lawyers, the judge, and a panel of my "peers" for three long months that, although there are parts of the night in question that I do not remember, I was in my hotel room for all of it. Sadly, my only alibi remains a bottle of whiskey. Again, not a good look. But who knew the earth was going to shift while I slept?

I have no idea how Mr. Haskins's sons ended up dead that night. Expensive lawyers, a need for a scapegoat in the face of extreme grief, and my own unwillingness to remember the deceased as better people than they appeared to me to be have colluded to seal my fate.

Haskins lost his family. His sons lost their lives. In a different way, I lost mine. Nobody won. That is all I remember. If you believe in justice, read no further.

MATTHEW P. MAYO is an award-winning author of more than thirty books and dozens of short stories. Find out more at matthewmayo.com.

Foreword to Lucky Tam's *A Tramp's Tales, or Episodes from the Life of a Rover*, annotated ed.

By Matthew P. Mayo

I N EARLY FEBRUARY 1952, while searching for a source of iridium in the Gila Wilderness in southwestern New Mexico, geologist Dr. Harvey Dinsmore IV happened upon a wad of ragged oilcloth wedged tight among boulders, seven feet up in a dry wash, barely above spring flood height. The humble bundle appeared to have been abandoned for years.

With much effort, the scientist tugged it free and unfolded the grimy cloth to reveal a weathered leather-covered book. In doing so, he unearthed one of the biggest mysteries of the last century: the legend of Lucky Tam. In the decades since Dr. Dinsmore began sharing the mysterious journal he found in that unlikely wilderness locale, historians and countless curious readers—among them scores of self-proclaimed "Tamblers"—have spent considerable effort in unraveling this enduring enigma.

Who was Lucky Tam? As author of the book—a diary, as it turns out—Tam partially answered that question by titling the work himself on the very first page: *A Tramp's Tales, or Episodes from the Life of a Rover*. That, however, would prove the extent of his assistance in the matter.

Scholars confidently maintain that his true identity has yet to be discovered, though various theories have been posited by researchers and Tam's readers.

According to critics, logic dictates the aforementioned Dr. Dinsmore may have been a huckster having a bit of fun at the public's expense. Yet Dinsmore had no history as a trickster, no personal motivation to foist an elaborate ruse on the public. Indeed, as a successful and respected research scientist, author, and lecturer, Dr. Harvey Dinsmore IV had every reason to avoid drawing such odd attentions as the journal brought him.

In an effort to mitigate the deleterious effects the Lucky Tam tome had on his reputation and career, Dr. Dinsmore donated the journal to the University of Washita at Cheyenne, Oklahoma. He hoped the gesture and the selection of a seemingly unbiased institution might reflect favorably on him, and further distance him from the suspicions of those who considered the discovery fraudulent.

When UW Press decided, in 1954, to publish the first official edition of *A Tramp's Tales*, Dinsmore agreed to lend his name to the project, by way of a brief introduction, in an effort to give the book a scholarly bent. The book sold well, and Dr. Dinsmore publicly announced he received no remuneration from its sale or his participation in it. However, his involvement in its release did little to lessen the damage, at least in scholarly circles, to his career. He had been heard on many occasions to utter regret over having "lugged the damnable diary back home with me."

In later years, Dr. Dinsmore managed to prop up his reputation with various geologic discoveries that proved beneficial to the US government's global military pursuits. And to his death in 1994 at age seventy-seven, in full retention of his faculties, Dr. Dinsmore proclaimed his innocence of what some wags referred to as "Dinsmore's Folly."

If we are to believe Lucky Tam's own brief biographical sketch, he was one of tens of thousands of young American men to return home, dazed and overwhelmed, from Europe and the madness of the First World War. According to Lucky Tam, these men were forever altered emotionally and physically by the filth of trench warfare, by the piercing whistle of artillery and the creeping poison of deadly gases, by the horrified screams of men reduced to blood and bone, "mewling for their mothers as they bled into muck, by death and rot, by questions without answer lasting a lifetime."

On his return to the United States and his hometown of "Filbert," Indiana, our hero eschews the life expected of him, and this is where the journal begins. Instead of settling down with his prewar sweetheart, "Lorena," and assuming his father's plumbing business, our everyman adopts the moniker "Lucky Tam" and takes to the road as a tramp with, as he writes, little more than "one slouch hat and the togs on my back, two good hands and a stout pair of boots, a dime-store diary with pencil enough for a short-stack of adventures."

By standards of the time, Lucky Tam lived a life of low-level hedonism—he smoked cigars and on occasion a corncob pipe, he drank when alcohol presented itself to him. He cut his own hair with a pocketknife that he kept "sharp as a crow's eye," he enjoyed whistling, and he paid for what material goods he required with that most base of currency, labor rendered by a strong mind and body.

That devil-may-care aura is the very reason I, like so many others, became attracted to the book. I first found Tam when I was a young, moody sort, prone to haunting the darkest corners of musty libraries and mildewed bookshops. It was in one such shop, the Mouse and Thimble, in Beasley, Massachusetts, in 1973, that I unearthed a tattered, much-taped copy of *A Tramp's Tales*. I read the words, I sensed the passion, and I smelled not mold and dust but the heady aroma of unfettered freedom as can only be envisaged by a youth with naught but possibility before him.

Years after my own discovery of Tam's journal, and after much roving, I found myself as a professor of literature, specializing in nineteenth- and twentieth-century American literary vagabonds, among them Walt Whitman, Jack London, Jack Kerouac, and none other than Lucky Tam. It is no surprise, then, and no coincidence, that I ended up heading the English department at the University of Washita. The position requires, in addition to various other duties, oversight of the UW Press, including its limited backlist titles, *A Tramp's Tales, or Episodes from the Life of a Rover* among them. Yes, I have access to the original battered leather-bound journal. And I have likely spent more time with it than the author himself.

In this revised and annotated second edition, we have restored the handful of minor passages omitted from the first, lines in which, admittedly, little of worth or revelation occur. Nonetheless, offered to the public for the first time is this complete version of the original diary, word for word, as set down by its author, Lucky Tam. Included also is Dr. Dinsmore's original introduction from 1954. (You'll note he now shares the dedication page with Lucky Tam, the man who made his life at times a vexation. I am unsure how the good doctor would feel about this, but I could not help myself.) Also included is half a century of research, commentary by leading Tam scholars, and margin notes revealing just what we know about this famous persona—and what remains a mystery.

Lucky Tam's fame comes not from being a returned warrior who tramped about and kept a diary. Indeed, he is not well known for any one exploit from his extraordinary life. Rather, he is remembered for the fact that he simply disappeared. As of this writing, no trace of the man (save for his journal) has been found.

Content-wise, we don't even know if Lucky Tam's diary is authentic. From a physical perspective, the journal itself has been verified by forensic analysis as authentic to the nine-year period the author's dated entries indicate. In addition, there exist a number of second- and thirdhand narrative accounts of people having met a man matching Tam's description and demeanor, and in the timeframe in which he mentions traveling the regions where the claimants dwelled.

Other clues indicating authenticity include common parlance of the times used by Tam in his entries, and various, albeit few, details sprinkled throughout his narratives about places and businesses he visited (the mercantile in West Knob, Wyoming, where he bartered labor for pencils and tobacco, for example).

There are also limited descriptions of the regiment with which he claimed to have been attached in the war, coupled with details of the war gleaned from his recountings of harrowing recurring nightmares. Historians of the Great War have offered insights and theories on which battles Tam may have seen and where his regiment may have been stationed.

Unfortunately, incomplete attempts have been made to account for each of the seventy-two returning men in his regiment. Likewise, investigations as to the whereabouts of his hometown ("Filbert" is another name for a hazelnut and is not, as it turns out, a town in Indiana), his intended fiancée, and his family and its plumbing business have proved fruitless.

And yet, there is the journal.

And there is the blood. Yes, blood—as yet lacking a DNA match—which has faded brown with time. And something else: stuck between pages in the diary is a bent feather, likely from the wing of a juvenile wild turkey (*Meleagris gallopavo*), with its quilly tip raggedly angled as if gnawed by teeth. The brown smears and the feather grimly decorating the pages of the last entry—photographed to be pictorially included in the published edition for the first time—provide intriguing clues as to the final days, hours, minutes, and seconds of Lucky Tam. We picture those teeth loosening in the puckered, bleeding mouth of a dying Tam.

Consider the diary's last passage, which follows the final dated entry—May 24, 1928, nine years from his first. Given the weak voice and weaker visual presentation of the entry itself, many readers have assumed Tam was scratching at death's door even as he scratched out these words:

> I aim to live, but how much longer? Bastid [sic] got me good. I don't know what it was, if it was man, beast, or other. Darkness hid it from me, but I

think it was starving. Its breath stank of fly-blown meat, of war. It grunted and snarled and savaged me with teeth like white knives. I expect it will be back, and I will not again be able to kick, nor shout it off. Dark is near, and I am bleeding from a mess of spots, most stopped but a few keep leaking, leaking out my last. My last . . . now think on that.

Tam's ever-present pencil apparently lost, devoted Tamblers maintain he had found the strength to transform the paltry feather into a utensil for scratching out his last words, rendered in his own blood, his savaged body as inkwell. Did the vicious attack Tam described take place upriver of where his cloth-wrapped journal was discovered, wedged and waiting? (Fortunate for us, if not for Dr. Dinsmore.) That is one explanation for the dearth of clues as to Tam's remains. The journal would have been the only marker of Tam's grave—if indeed he died after writing one last entry.

Odd as it sounds, it is possible there are some still unfamiliar with the enigmatic author and his riveting diary. That makes this new edition, revised with updated footnotes, commentary, photographs, and historical addenda, so much more special. The intention of this exhaustive volume was to attempt to answer the myriad questions that have surrounded Tam's journal since its discovery all those years ago. And yet we still find ourselves with more questions than answers—not that we mind.

The enduring appeal of the legend of Lucky Tam is its mystery, and people savor mysteries. We like their challenge, and we relish when conundrums foil our best efforts at solving them. Lucky Tam has proved to be among the twentieth century's penultimate pickles, the very cause of his enduring appeal to sleuths trained and homespun—anyone, in fact, who has ever yearned to chuck it all, walk away, and never look back. Tam will forever remain alive in the gripping, ragged pages of his journal, fabricated or no. For it represents a hope, an ideal, a life most of us yearn for yet will never live.

I leave it to you, reader, to sift wheat from chaff, to kick the can down your own mysterious dirt road, and decide if Lucky Tam was indeed a strange character of Dr. Dinsmore's making, or a huckster bent on shamming the finders of conjured diary entries, or if he was, as is believed by many, honest and real and true.

And so I ask again, who was Lucky Tam? We may know. Or we may never know. In the end, does it matter?

Matthew P. Mayo

Autumn 2017

JOHN PAUL WHITE (@johnpaulwhite) is a Grammy Award–winning singer-songwriter and former member of the duo the Civil Wars.

Foreword to *The Killens: Monstrosity and Murder at the Infamous Traveling Carnival and Sideshow*, by Barbara Lewis Beauregard

By John Paul White

ISAAC WHITE wasn't like the other boys.

He didn't have the same hopes and dreams. He never fantasized about hitting the winning home run. He paid no attention to the homecoming queen, much less coveted her. He held no aspirations for Hollywood, or big city lights in general.

He just wanted to blend in. He wanted to be with people who understood his plight, carried his burden, bore his shame. He wanted to be judged for what was inside—instead of what was out.

And Isaac had a plan.

In the Depression-era South, carnivals blew in on the wind and then disappeared just as quickly. They were an escape for the lucky ticket holders . . . but also for those desperate to leave their hopeless, dead-end lives behind. They offered an opportunity to shake the dust off your feet and ride the rails with other like-minded wanderers.

But there was one carnival that was different from the others. Much different. It spread curiosity, fear, and outright horror.

For Isaac, it was perfect.

Born with twisted limbs and facial abnormalities, my great-great-uncle Isaac was an old and often overlooked leaf on our family tree. In fact, no one in my family knew Isaac's full story until the historian Barbara Lewis Beauregard reached out to his descendants—including me—to ask for help researching one of the performers at the now-infamous Killens Traveling Carnival and Sideshow. We discovered Isaac's journal in a stash of family photo albums and documents, though it ultimately left us with more questions than answers, and Ms. Beauregard was forced to piece together much of the story from newspaper clippings and other townspeople's accounts.

At the turn of the twentieth century, there were around twenty traveling carnivals in the United States, inspired by the success of the Chicago World's Fair in 1893. By the late 1930s, there were an estimated three hundred carnivals touring the country, no two quite the same but all boasting some mix of circus, vaudeville, burlesque, and magic—and freak sideshows. It was into this world that my great-great-uncle disappeared . . . around the time of a string of brutal murders that shocked the sleepy rural town nearby.

What you're about to read is a cautionary tale. At its center is this hard fact: sometimes what makes us the same . . . is what makes us very different.

SHIRLEY MANSON (@garbage) is a Grammy-nominated artist—the lead singer of Garbage, a songwriter, actress, advocate, and overall badass.

Foreword to Alanna Trask's *Keep Your Gaze on Me: A True Story of Social Media, Obsession, and Murder*

By Shirley Manson

WITH HER CONTROVERSIAL NEW BOOK *Keep Your Gaze on Me*, internationally renowned intersectional feminist Alanna Trask explores the infamous abduction and brutal murder of media star Persia Sadsashay. The crime not only shocked a generation but also drew much-needed attention to the heartbreaking trend of self-objectification by underage teens in our society.

As has been widely reported by the media, drifter Bo Don Coy abducted Sadsashay from her Los Angeles home in broad daylight, leaving behind a series of terrifying pornographic images painted in blood on the walls of his victim's bedroom. Under cover of darkness, he later broke into Disneyland and positioned her body in a macabre tableau, manipulating her corpse into a seated position inside one of the teacups on the Mad Tea Party ride.

Fifty-nine-year-old Don Coy was a behavioral addict. Nursing an unhealthy fixation with both pornography and guns, he quickly spiraled out of control upon arriving in Los Angeles from the relative backwoods of Terre Haute, Indiana, six months before the murder.

For reasons yet to be fully understood, Don Coy had grown obsessed with the young Sadsashay, who shot to fame after streaming, at the age of thirteen, a bewilderingly bizarre pornographic performance on Snapchat. The video offended Middle America but turned her into a household name overnight.

In this chilling and provocative book, Alanna Trask examines the cultural climate at the time of Sadsashay's murder, launching a crucial conversation that needs to be continued about the normalization of hypersexualized minors in the music and fashion industries, in Hollywood, and on social media. Trask poses some hard questions concerning the ascent of the fourteen-year-old who described herself as the "Perfect Slut."

Are the companies who fall over themselves to sign minors to endorsement deals complicit in their exploitation or are they merely profiting from it?

What part, if any, did Sadsashay's sixteen million followers play in her murder?

What changes in the law can be made to protect our children from predators and unwanted attention online? How do we teach them to navigate a world that has developed a disturbing taste in increasingly young "stars" who are hungry for attention?

Keep Your Gaze on Me is a dark book with a fittingly solemn and challenging narrative. It is admittedly difficult to stomach in places. Trask is a skilled storyteller, however, presenting such a fascinating dissection of our sociological pathology that it makes for a riveting read. I couldn't put it down, and neither will you.

5

Pop Culture and Fandom

COME OUT AND COSPLAY

FANDOM IS AT A FEVER PITCH for just about any genre. There seem to be "cons" for everything, with cosplay taking off everywhere you go. At Comic-Con, it's not uncommon to find Darth Vader walking around with a Sailor Moon girl trying to get a *Game of Thrones* star's autograph. And it's not just the Marvel universe that can boast hordes of devoted superfans. Our passion for all things pop extends to binge-watching just about everything from *Real Housewives* to *Barry*. Life can be stressful, and we need escape. Good news for us: with content so readily available, we can get our fix as often as we want. And this chapter plays right into it. It's for the fanboys and fangirls out there. You'll read about the dead walking, men in tights, women in Beverly Hills, and places people have boldly gone before. We promise this section won't wander too far off into the woods like Carl and his hair did on *The Walking Dead*; it won't keep you waiting like those post-credits scenes in your favorite Marvel film. What it will do is just about quench your pop-culture thirst and leave you wanting more.

GEORGE GENE GUSTINES has worked at the *New York Times* since 1990. He began writing about comics in 2002. His career goals are landing a comics story on the front page and working for the *Times* until at least 2030.

Foreword to Bethany Snow's *Remembering Comic Books: The Never-Ending Story Concludes*

By George Gene Gustines

H AS IT REALLY BEEN a hundred years since the birth of the comic book industry? (Relax, fellow nerds, we know that comics predate Superman's 1938 arrival, *we know*. Yet despite the phenomenal success of the Image Comics streaming service, whose slogan is "No Capes / No Clothing," to the general public, comics = superheroes, so *deal with it*.) And while the shutdown of the industry in 2028 was acknowledged at the time in the country's handful of remaining newspapers and magazines, it takes a little distance—in this case, ten years—to step back, ruminate, and analyze the (mostly) glorious end to a true American art form.

That is exactly what *Remembering Comic Books: The Never-Ending Story Concludes* accomplishes, and I am honored to have been asked to introduce readers to this important retrospective. Though nonfiction, the book almost reads like a Brad Meltzer thriller, the tone set from the opening line: "Everyone thought comic books would always be safe." (By "everyone," of course, Ms. Snow means the "minutia-obsessed fans that considered such weighty matters." She definitely has an old-school view of comics fandom.)

But with all due respect, we fans of comic books—and I truly mean books, not the TV and movie adaptations—there had long been signs of this decline. The Johnny Storms-come-lately paid these signs no mind. Especially not the puppet masters behind the mega corporations who profited from the characters, who leaped from the pages to appear in films, TV shows, cartoons, restaurants, two-year universities, Zambonis, amusement parks, airlines, children's hospitals, vacation resorts, law firms, voting machines, and so on. The puppet masters eventually realized new material no longer mattered.

After all, why bother creating original stories when the masses were enraptured with the annual reboots of their favorite hero's origin story? Moviegoers had embraced three different *Spider-Man* origin stories in just fifteen years between 2002 and 2017; it seemed only justified to keep going back to the same wells.

Unfortunately, as millions of ticket buyers marched into theaters to see comic characters on the big screen, only hardcore hundreds of readers were buying the books. (One of the saddest parts of *Remembering Comics* are the 2023 to 2026 charts of devastatingly low sales.) As Ms. Snow adeptly argues, the pivotal lesson for comic book publishers came in 2017, long before the precipitous book sales decline. Thanks, Hollywood!

Ms. Snow reports that 2017 saw a record number of comic-related properties that were adapted for theaters, TV, or digital series. But the most critical releases were *Wonder Woman*, which told the beginning of the journey for the hero (played by Gal Gadot), and *Logan*, which chronicled the *end* of the franchise. (And what a conclusion!) Tellingly, showing the end of the story for the hunky, hairy, and beloved Wolverine made the film one of the most critically acclaimed superhero movies of the era. It showed that the makers could create a nova blast by chronicling the definitive final chapters of their intellectual properties. (Yes, my fellow geeks, *I know* DC and Marvel had experimented with this before, hence the rolling of my eyes, but they were seen as "Elseworlds" and "What If" stories—as if any of these stories were real.) The age of geek reached its apex the next month with Gal Gadot and Hugh Jackman on that Oscar night.

Still, for a few years, comic publishers, predictably, continued to focus on beginnings. However, as comic publishers ever so slowly realized there was no need to continue the stories of multimedia successes like Cloud, Freedom Ring, Jack Knight, Shirtless Bear Fighter, and Sideways, they got wise. And the precipitous sales decline that began in 2023 got them to take a closer look at lessons that *Logan* and *Avengers 4* should've imparted years before: audiences LOVE conclusions. And, great Caesar's ghost, dedicated comic *readers* were going to get them!

Some of the endings were mean-spirited, and Ms. Snow seems to delight in highlighting them in the second part of this book. One of her favorites: the reveal that Captain America died of hypothermia in 1945 and that his discovery by the Avengers and all that followed for decades after were the delusions of a dying man. She also takes particular glee at the final chapter for Superman. While a strong case can be made that Clark Kent breached ethical codes of journalism by reporting on the exploits of the Man of Steel, it felt extremely petty to have Superman outed by a *Daily Planet* accountant who wondered why Mr. Kent, who often found himself in the most exotic locales for his bylines, never filed for reimbursement. Foiled by the Menace of the Middle Manager!

On a side note, who knew that the Marvel and DC rivalry would be settled the way it did? Once both publishers, and their parent companies, were purchased by Amazon, fanboys got every crossover they thought they wanted—and the ability to have the toy tie-ins delivered by drone along with their Trident, Snapple, and Xanax. And the capitalistic synergy was inspired; it was genius to turn *American Idol* into a search for the next star of the live-action *Dazzler* film. Monstrous TV viewership led to a legion of music downloads, which created an avalanche at the box office.

The final age of comics was grand and showed how much the actual books had been once again embraced by the country. Getting Mark Ruffalo to pen "This Is Our Hulk," the end of the green giant, was a brilliant move and his soulful monologues even brought tears to the eyes of Ms. Snow. The verbose (and Pulitzer-winning) Brian Michael Bendis opting to write and draw the hundred-page, dialogue-free goodbye to the mute Jericho? Magical! The writing team of Tina Fey and Seth Meyers on Animal Man's and Squirrel Girl's final battle against animal poachers? An absolute tearjerker (and the money it raised for the World Wildlife Fund was staggering).

I could go on, but instead I'll allow *Remembering Comic Books* to tell you the whole story. After you finish this inspiring book, I invite you to revisit what we once called the "source material." Download one of those tremendous last wills and testaments and, for one moment and for one last time, allow yourself to "Just Imagine."

JAYSON STARK has covered baseball for more than thirty years, for ESPN and the *Philadelphia Inquirer*. He is the author of three baseball books, is a two-time Pennsylvania sportswriter of the year, and was honored in 2010 by Penn State's Foster Conference for Distinguished Writers. In 2019, Stark was the recipient of the Baseball Hall of Fame's J.G. Taylor Spink Award for meritorious contributions to baseball writing.

Foreword to Clark Kent's *Behind the Iron Curtain: The Unauthorized Biography of Tony Stark*

By Jayson Stark

I T MIGHT SEEM STRANGE that I, a sportswriter, should write the foreword to the unauthorized bio of Tony Stark because, let's face it—I'm his least authorized cousin. But I'm given to understand that none of Tony's associates were willing to step up to the plate (I heard a rumor they balked because of who the author is, and not just because Tony wasn't involved with the writing; they seem to have some sort of weird rivalry going on with Kent). I, on the other hand, am always happy to help a fellow journalist, so here we are.

Everywhere I go, people are always asking me about Tony—is it true we're related? I proudly brag that yes, actually, I'm his cousin. And every darned one of those people seems to find that amusing. Who knows why.

I have to admit there's one thing about the fixation with Tony that always bothers me. I can't figure out why you never hear or read a word about Tony's brief but mesmerizing baseball career. (Heck, the author even left it out of this book. That's kind of like writing a bio of John Stamos and never mentioning his hair. Isn't it?) Granted, I'm a guy who has spent his life hanging out with more baseball players than superheroes, so I might be more into the sport than Tony's average fan. But you'd think *someone* would have been interested in it before now.

So, I'm glad for this opportunity to correct this grievous oversight, in an unauthorized kind of way. It's crazy to think that everyone believes Tony got into MIT at age fifteen because he had qualities like brains and more money than Bill Gates. The truth is, practically from the first time he grabbed a bat, the dude could hit a breaking ball like no one we've ever seen. At MIT, where I'm pretty sure that term "spin rate" was invented, the coaches used to talk about Tony the way the rest of New England talked about Ted Williams.

Hitting isn't just about hand-eye coordination, you know. It's about pitch recognition. And with Tony's supremo vision, it didn't matter if you threw him a curve, a slider, a cutter, a splitter, a screwball, a two-seamer, a four-seamer, a slurve, a palmball, a forkball, a knuckleball, or a pitch you just made up in the middle of your windup. He could spot it like four inches out of your hand. I remember he'd stand in the box and shout out what pitch was coming before it got within fifty feet of the plate. It was the damnedest thing I've ever seen. And it drove pitchers wacko. Imagine trying to set up a hitter for a two-strike slider, after not throwing a slider the whole frigging game. And now you snap that sucker off, only to hear the dude at home plate go, "Slider. On it. Watch out. It's coming back at you, twice as hard as you threw it."

Tony can be cocky like that. You might have heard stories about that—there have been lots of times when Tony's ego created some problems with his team. (If you haven't heard those stories, check out chapters five through fifteen of this book.) They just never involved his *baseball* team.

I swear Tony batted something like .718 against breaking balls in his freshman year, until—well, we'll get to that later. That year, I even convinced my buddy Peter Gammons to bring the Red Sox over to watch him hit on off days. Tony got pretty tight with Wade Boggs, who had just joined the team the year before. Wade once told Gammons, "If I could have learned to hit a curve ball like that when

I was fifteen, I'd have gotten four thousand hits, not three thousand." (*Sports Illustrated* actually cut that quote out of one of Peter's notes columns. If *Sports Illustrated* had put Tony Stark, the Greatest Fifteen-Year-Old Hitter Alive, on the cover, Tony might have wound up in Cooperstown instead of with the Knights of the Atomic Round Table. And the world as we know it would be totally different.)

Still, once you read about Tony's exploits and his, well, troublesome attitude, you won't be shocked that he never took baseball seriously enough to generate the kind of buzz that would have gotten him to the big leagues. He'd miss practice three or four days a week, and you never knew if it was because he was off playing chess or if he was just out somewhere enjoying his favorite beverage. But he was the best hitter on the team. And he always showed up before games to hand out copies of the other team's scouting reports. So the coaches kept letting him slide.

But about halfway through that season, he just up and vanished from the team. Never showed up for another practice, another game, not even a team party with the girls from Tufts. The official story is that he lost interest, needed to spend more time studying . . . yada yada yada. That can't be all there was to it, but I'm his cousin and even I didn't get the whole story. Maybe there's something in Kent's chapter on Tony at MIT, but he focuses more on Tony's grades and his budding friendship with James Rhodes.

Anyway, Tony has gone on to have an amazing life. The kind of life people make movies about. But any time people ask me about him, I can't help but think about what might have been. Studs who can hit a baseball the way he could hit a baseball don't come along very often.

Close your eyes and envision that alternate universe, with an actual superhero standing at home plate, screaming out every pitch they threw him at the top of his lungs, hitting baseballs where only superheroes can hit them. Off fences. Off light towers. Off skyscrapers. Off airplanes ill-advisedly passing over the ballpark.

That could have been Tony.

Of course, had Tony stayed on the team the country might have been destroyed many times over by now, so even though I'll always wish Tony had transformed the world of baseball the way he transformed the rest of the world, it's probably for the best.

You're about to read about all the other amazing stuff he went on to do. And maybe I'm too focused on that short episode in Tony's past, but I think it means something that so many great athletes seem to share a secret drive, a passion for a bigger purpose. If the story of Tony's baseball career were told more often, maybe more of our athletes would also be celebrated for the ways they've worked to save the world. (And they didn't necessarily trade their uniforms for super-powered suits to do it.)

Maybe you don't believe a word of this. Can't say I blame you. But I couldn't let this volume roll off the presses without letting you in on Tony Stark, the kid who perfected the perfect baseball swing long before he perfected his legendary repulsor ray.

JERRY SPRINGER (@jerryspringer) is a syndicated talk show host, former politician, and news anchor. He has hosted his talk show, *The Jerry Springer Show*, since 1991.

Foreword to *Fly Ball: How the New York Yankees Have Changed Lives*, a compilation

By Jerry Springer

I REALIZE WHEN YOU THINK of the most storied franchise in sports history, I might not be the most logical person to write the foreword to a book subtitled *How the New York Yankees Have Changed Lives*. I'm the former mayor of Cincinnati and have hosted my own show for twenty-plus years, but it makes sense. Trust me. When you look a bit closer, you'll see a stronger connection between me and the pinstripes.

Forget changing lives. The New York Yankees may have *saved* mine.

My family came to this country from England back in 1950, fleeing as German refugees during the war. When we arrived here, I immediately stuck out like a sore thumb. I spoke with an English accent, and my mom, well, she dressed me as if we never left England. I had my blue shorts, jacket, bow tie, and knee-high socks on as I walked into school on my first day. Oh, and I wore a beret. Yes, a beret.

Needless to say, I got my ass kicked. My mom even asked other mothers in the school how I might avoid the beatings and gain some respect from my classmates. A trip to a department store changed my experience—and my life really. Under the advice of the other mothers, my mom picked up a Yankee uniform with the number 8 emblazoned on the back, and all of a sudden, one outfit stopped me from being a punching bag.

My alignment with Yogi Berra made me fit right in, and my fandom for the Bronx Bombers has never wavered since. I live and breathe this team—through the best of the best years to the worst of the worst.

I have even played in fantasy camps alongside players I'd idolized, from number 8 himself to "the Mick" to Mickey Rivers. I even caught Whitey Ford one time with Mantle at the plate. I remember it vividly; I was practically shaking. Whitey himself had to calm me down, easing my nerves by telling me "the Mick" had been out of the game for nearly two decades and was tipsy.

That was the closest I felt to having made it to "the bigs"—though I must admit those "Jeee'rrry! Jeee'rrry!" chants I get at my show feel pretty good, too. When I'm about to enter the studio audience I almost feel like I'm walking to the batter's box.

Putting on pinstripes is a sense of pride for so many baseball players through history. For me, it really saved my life and changed the course of it. So read on. You'll discover how the Yankees have changed the lives of fans, rivals, and an entire city.

Some sentiments of this story were shared in a May 4, 2011, ESPN.com article written by Thomas Neumann.

KERRY CAHILL is an actress whose credits include *The Walking Dead*, *Terminator Genisys*, and *Now You See Me*.

Foreword to *Walkers, Survivors, and Aiming for the Head in Our Modern-Day Zombie Apocalypse*, by Tom Smith, former army captain and CIA field agent

By Kerry Cahill

W E ALL LOVE ZOMBIES, love to hate them, love to pretend to kill them, and even love to dress up as them. It is no secret that we all have a hypothetical "zombie apocalypse team," and we all know which of our friends are (and aren't) on it.

As a fan of zombie movies and zombie lore, Captain Tom Smith knows that these tales are often allegories for real-life crises. This book is about the zombie apocalypse in which we are currently living. Not an outbreak of literal zombies, but a problem of our collective psyche. *Walkers, Survivors, and Aiming for the Head* is an investigation into American psychology.

Just as the characters in any zombie story must reckon with their own humanity, so, too, must we.

Smith walks us through the symptoms of our current plague: the rising obesity rates, the death of political civility, and social media obsessions. And, more important, he offers a scathing look at our individual roles in each of these problems. Using his own personal stories as well as those of successful and unsuccessful public figures, Smith analyzes how we put together our own "survival teams," who we are on those teams, and why we will ultimately succeed or fail. Smith's words made me take a hard look at my own chances of survival. Friends, this book is a wake-up call.

This is a book about the zombie in you. A book about who you are when you look in the mirror in the morning, how you choose to walk out of the house every day, and how your action (or inaction) may affect the world.

As a former CIA field agent, Smith has a special perspective into how we may escape our possible destiny of war and struggle. Tom's military past has brought him face-to-face with the abyss, and we as readers get to know how he walked away intact.

I am proud to call Tom a friend and even prouder to know him after reading this. Tom is asking Americans to look in the mirror and take accountability. This is no small ask. This is a book that needs to be thoroughly chewed, not quickly swallowed. It is not an easy read, but when you make it to the end, your world will be forever changed.

DAN EPSTEIN (@BigHairPlasGras) is the author of the 1970s baseball histories *Big Hair and Plastic Grass: A Funky Ride through Baseball and America in the Swinging '70s* and *Stars and Strikes: Baseball and America in the Bicentennial Summer of '76.* He writes about baseball, music, and other cultural obsessions for a variety of outlets, including *Rolling Stone, Revolver,* and *October.*

Foreword to Wink Martindale's *High Rollers: In the Spotlight and Behind the Scenes in the Golden Age of TV Game Shows*

By Dan Epstein

AUGUST 1975. *Jaws* is breaking box-office records, "Jive Talkin'" by the Bee Gees is blasting out of every radio, and the sudden disappearance of former Teamsters Union president Jimmy Hoffa is the talk of every news broadcast. And I'm out of my mind with excitement because my mom is taking my sister and me to the CBS Television City complex in Los Angeles, where we're going to be part of the studio audience for a taping of *Gambit*, a blackjack-themed game show hosted by Wink Martindale . . .

From the standpoint of our present era, when we're all suffering to some extent from extreme media inundation, it probably seems a bit absurd that I would have been so unbelievably amped to attend the taping of a TV game show. But back in the pre-cable mid-'70s, network television was a huge part of my life, and even my identity; long before my friends and I defined ourselves by the music we listened to or the sports teams we rooted for, we defined ourselves by the TV shows we watched. And while I loved most of the same sitcoms and cop shows that my friends did, I was the only one in our little group who was completely obsessed with game shows.

Maybe it was a by-product of all the summer months I'd spent visiting my grandparents in Alabama; the brutal heat and thick humidity kept me inside during the peak hours of the day, and game shows seemed a far more compelling option for air-conditioned daytime TV viewing than my grandma's soap operas. Or maybe it was the way that a game show's flashing lights, ringing bells, whooping contestants, cheering audiences, and peppy bursts of Tijuana Brass–inspired music combined to deliver bite-sized doses of the sort of giddy excitement I'd only previously experienced at carnivals or amusement parks.

Game show hosts seemed to occupy a unique substratum of the Hollywood pantheon. They were demigods, able to casually joke and interact with the celebrities who appeared on their programs, yet also capable of radiating enough charm and regular-guy bonhomie to put their contestants at ease—and they all seemed to talk, look, and dress like your slightly groovy uncle. And for me, Wink Martindale was the epitome of the classic game show host.

That's why I was surprised and pleased when Wink reached out to me to pen the foreword to this book; though millennials and younger readers may not have heard of him, Wink was as much of a household name as Bob Barker or Alex Trebek. And though he could have had any number of current game show hosts write this, Wink said he wanted a different point of view to introduce this book. Rather than another host, or even a contestant, he wanted someone else: a one-time member of his studio audience. I was only too happy to accept.

I learned a lot on that epic afternoon and evening in August 1975, when my mom, sister, and I sat through the taping of three consecutive *Gambit* episodes. (And for the first time in my life, I felt myself experiencing an interest in Mexican food, thanks to the Taco Bell spots that were screened incessantly during the commercial breaks.)

Like so many viewers, I was transfixed by Wink Martindale. There were no celebrity guests on *Gambit*, but he had more than enough star power to compensate—and yet, he was also disarmingly warm and down-to-earth in his interactions with the couples who appeared on the show that day. I didn't know at the time that he was a showbiz lifer who had begun a lengthy radio career as a seventeen-year-old disc jockey in Jackson, Tennessee, or that he'd scored a top ten hit in 1959 with a spoken word single called "Deck of Cards." I didn't know that he'd hosted two previous game shows (*What's This Song?* and *Words and Music*) before *Gambit*, and of course I had no way of knowing that he'd go on to even greater success with the mighty *Tic-Tac-Dough*. All I knew was that this guy was clearly in his element, smoothly handling every cue, retake, and set change with the ease of a seasoned pro, and cracking wise with the audience and contestants whenever there was a lull in the action.

Four decades later, Wink Martindale brings that same smooth assurance and easygoing wit to this nostalgic and insightful look at the golden age of game shows. He takes us behind the scenes at tapings, where we'll discover game show secrets, like that everyone appearing on the show had to change clothes between episodes in order to make each episode appear as if it were happening on a new day. To hear Wink tell it, the set of a game show was a far less exciting, joyous, and glamorous place than most of us imagine. There were altercations with producers, grumpy contestants, and days when he just felt too tired. As I learned from my day there, spontaneous reactions from the studio audience were completely frowned upon, so you had to keep your eye on the "Applause" signs, which would light up whenever the producers wanted you to clap, and otherwise keep your mouth shut and your arms by your sides. But as Wink explains, sometimes audience members didn't obey, and security had to be called. Wink was *there*, man; he knows how it all went down, and he's here to take us through it.

However, for all that it shines a stark spotlight on the unglamorous realities behind the game show glitz, *High Rollers* still celebrates all the magic and excitement of those flashing lights and that frenetic music. To many of us, living in the brown corduroy drabness of Middle America, the modern-day gods of the Hollywood Olympus were remote and untouchable, and we could only commune with them at the theater or in my family's TV room. But game shows were the one place where we could see mere mortals—the contestants—actually interacting with Hollywood deities, and there was something incredibly life affirming about that. It didn't matter that the celebrities who populated the panels of shows like *Hollywood Squares* or *Match Game* were actually B- (or even C-) listers, or that Paul Lynde wasn't really as famous as, say, Paul Newman; if they were famous (or funny) enough to land a game show gig, they were sufficiently Olympian to us.

I can think of no better host than Wink for a journey back to this golden age. Enjoy the ride.

BILLY YOST (@billyghost) is a musician in the Chicago indie rock band the Kickback.

Foreword to *I Did Not Realize That Constituted Stalking: Fandom for the New Millennium*, edited by Sheila Ruminard

By Billy Yost

I T IS NOT DIFFICULT to assume that my rather well-publicized arrest and *extremely minimal* period of incarceration provided me a sort of unfortunate top-contender status to open this collection. But I've been told that I can write what I please, and I'm grateful to editor Sheila Ruminard for the opportunity to maybe explain myself just a little bit, here in the opening pages of *I Did Not Realize That Constituted Stalking: Fandom for the New Millennium*.

While there is a lot that can be said about the events of October 27, 2014, there are a few facts that I believe bear repeating. First, at no point was esteemed (though surprisingly short) actor Michael Keaton in danger. Not even for a moment. Despite exaggerated reports from multiple press organizations, my ushering Mr. Keaton into my car while wearing a finely made prop replica utility belt (from Tim Burton's 1989 tour de force and genre-defining film *Batman*) did not constitute a safety crisis, let alone armed kidnapping. Furthermore, those few pedestrians who sought to intervene in what was clearly a personal matter between Mr. Keaton and me should feel great shame. My comments made to them through an admittedly cheap Dark Knight cowl (not technically based on the 1989 Batsuit design, but still conducive for the purposes relayed here and in legal record of note) could not remotely be interpreted as what the Los Angeles Superior Court later deemed "terroristic in intent and purpose." I was merely repeating some of Keaton's clutch dialogue from the aforementioned film. "Come on! Let's get nuts" isn't even that threatening.

There is not enough space allocated here for me to fully explain myself, the subsequent low-speed chase, or Mr. Keaton's unwillingness to grant that he kind of seemed to be having a good time, and so I think it important to merely say here that being a fan is hard. But wasn't it Batman who taught us the crucial lesson that "Someone has to do it"?

If you or someone you love shares a story like mine, or frenzied night-sweating fantasies of eventually having a story like mine, that's where this book may come in handy. While on the surface, these might look like collected cautionary tales of overzealous fandom serialized for bathroom reading, I hope you, dear reader, might see them for the love stories they are. Take, for example, Quincy Yakov, the middle-aged Oregonian who attempted to pass for an elementary-aged extra in *Kindergarten Cop* in order to collect Arnold Schwarzenegger's nail clippings. Or teenager Yuma Keeling attempting to physically mail herself to Lil Yachty's weirdly non-maritime-themed home. In these and many other stories, some may see chaos, but a few of us will see perfect order—order that Batman would respect.

[Legal counsel for the collected stakeholders of this anthology would like to reassert that in no way should this foreword read as an endorsement of Mr. Yost's actions or of any other illegal behavior described in this book.]

JORDAN ELIZABETH FAZIO is a comedy writer, whose work (namely games involving drag queens and sexual puns) could be seen nightly on Bravo's late-night TV show *Watch What Happens Live with Andy Cohen* and was a frequent guest on SiriusXM's *Radio Andy*. Before that, she wrote questions for ABC's *Who Wants to Be a Millionaire?*, which only sometimes included sexual puns, and was a witty and whimsical staple on the NYC comedy circuit for many years. Jordan has lately given up stand-up to focus on raising her actor husband, Anthony, and their son, Cooper.

Foreword to Sir Anthony Hopkins's *The Real Housewives: A Definitive History*

By "Sir Ian McKellen"

D EAR READER,
I am probably just as shocked as you are that renowned actor and esteemed member of the Most Excellent Order of the British Empire Sir Anthony Hopkins asked me to write the foreword to this book. But as a fellow *Real Housewives* fan, this was truly an honor. Few people know that Sir Anthony is a devout follower of *The Real Housewives* and deeply emotionally invested in every franchise (New Jersey being the exception—Sir Anthony finds the fact that half of the women's husbands are named "Joe" far too confusing). In fact, we spend hours after each meeting of the knights dissecting the intricacies of the women's feuds and discussing who our fellow knights are most like (Anthony is such a Bethenny. Me? I'm obviously a Lisa Vanderpump).

Now in his golden years, Sir Anthony has focused his creative efforts less on acting and more on this deep dive into the illustrious history of *The Real Housewives*. Traveling to the eye of the botox-injected storms of Atlanta, Beverly Hills, Orange County, New York, Dallas, and Potomac over the course of four years, Sir Anthony has put together the most in-depth oral history of the television show that gave women with so little to say the platform to say so much. From the casting couch and beyond, Sir Anthony delves deep into the thoughtlessness that preceded such iconic events as Sheree pulling Kim's wig, and Lisa Rinna asking Dorit if she was doing coke at a dinner party six months prior while the rest of the group talked about what deep fears keep them awake at night.

When my dear friend Sir Anthony announced he was writing this book—or rather, when a "friend" leaked it to the media (I won't print her name, lest we start drama, but let's call her "Lame Moody Wench")—he was widely ridiculed. The *Daily Mail* said he had gone off the deep end. The *Mirror* insinuated he was on the drink. I, however, am more than happy to come to his defense. I ask you, who among us doesn't have a show that we just can't quit (and wouldn't want to even if we could)? Though she won't admit it, "Moody" loves the Housewives franchise, too. I can attest that she and I have kiki'd over the dissolution of Bethenny and Carole's friendship many times over. We all need an escape; that pretend group of gal pals on your TV to share of glass of Chardonnay with (or throw at Eileen Davidson, if you're Brandi Glanville—amirite?!).

In this book, Sir Anthony shares his not-so-guilty pleasure with you and lets you in on our little fireside chats. He gives you his unfiltered opinions on pivotal dramatic moments, such as Alexis Bellino accusing Vicki of being into threesomes while they skied and that time Brandi Glanville told musical artist Babyface that the way he played guitar looked like he was "finger banging" his wife (spoiler: Sir Anthony thought it was uproariously funny, albeit inaccurate).

In the following pages, Sir Anthony also fearlessly divulges that this secret passion has seeped into his acting process. While preparing for roles such as the titular monarch in BBC's *King Lear*, Hopkins drew inspiration of a father's descent into madness and pitting his daughters against each other from Yolanda Hadid, momager to her two supermodel daughters, who clearly prefers her eldest, Gigi, to the broodier Bella. One can only wonder how his turn as Hannibal

Lecter might have been elevated had NY housewife Jill Zarin been there on his TV screen to inspire the character's desire to eat human flesh with a smile.

This book may not change your mind on *The Real Housewives*, but it certainly will change how you look at one of the greatest actors of our time. Eat your heart out, Judi!

AL SNOW is a former ECW and WWE professional wrestler, trainer, actor, host of WWE's *Tough Enough*, and the CEO and founder of the wrestling apparel brand COLLARxELBOW.

Foreword to Simon Phillips's *The Wind Beneath My Wings: Celebrities on Their Heroes, Mentors, and Guiding Lights*

By Al Snow

THEY SAY NEVER MEET YOUR HEROES. The thinking, of course, is that the reality can never match the fantasy. That may hold true for most, but not if your hero is Patrick Duffy.

I first encountered Patrick Duffy on NBC's television series *Man from Atlantis*. Thanks to his immense skills in the art of acting, Patrick adeptly portrayed a man from Atlantis. Complete with gills, webbed toes, and hands to allow him to swim in an undulating, Slinky-ish, seizure-like fashion.

It was truly breathtaking to watch.

Patrick was so blessed by the muse of acting that he made you believe he could actually breathe underwater. It made you want to swim just like he did. (Unfortunately, that actually got me kicked out of my local public pool when fellow swimmers lodged a lewdness complaint with the lifeguard.) Thanks to *Man from Atlantis*, Patrick was poised to be launched into superstardom, but alas, it was not to be.

NBC foolishly canceled the series, and Patrick Duffy disappeared from my life.

I had only seen one other man ever display the same talent for the thespian arts as did young Patrick Duffy. His name was Simon Mac-Corkindale, or as we like to call him, the Cork. Simon had his own amazing series on NBC titled *Manimal*. Much like what happened to my hero, Patrick, as Simon stood on the precipice of greatness, NBC also blindly canceled *Manimal.*

Many years went by with my trying to grasp exactly why NBC seemed to have a witch hunt against such incredibly talented individuals as my hero, Patrick, and the Cork. But then one night I spied on CBS a series called *Dallas,* and what did my longing eyes see? My hero had returned to the small screen as Bobby Ewing. This role didn't have the depth of the man from Atlantis but Patrick again went on to master the intricacies of the character and overcome the challenges of creating passionate and believable love scenes with his costar Victoria Principal. I could even see him paying homage to his old character in those scenes by emulating his classic swimming technique under the covers. Well played, Patrick—thumbing your nose at NBC and their folly for canceling *Man from Atlantis.*

Patrick played the character so well that when he stood on the very edge of greatness once more, CBS attempted to follow NBC's vendetta against great acting and wrote a scene where Patrick's character Bobby Ewing was shot and killed. But this time, the legions of Patrickmaniacs (as we like to call ourselves) said, "We're not just going to sit back and allow this to happen to the Duffster." No, sir. We petitioned CBS nonstop, and some of us even threatened to kidnap certain executives' families and children if Patrick Duffy were no longer on the show.

Thanks to our efforts—and, of course, Patrick Duffy's immeasurable talent—CBS acquiesced and through some great TV writing the shooting was recast as only a dream sequence. Huzzah!!! My hero was safely ensconced in the annals of television history where he rightfully belonged.

I have spent years enjoying my hero Patrick Duffy's talents on TV, but I'd been careful to follow the advice I stated at the start of this foreword about being careful not to meet your heroes. But this book made me rethink that old advice. Here, dozens of celebrities from Meryl Streep to Stone Cold Steve Austin tell stories about the people who inspire them, and how meeting their heroes changed their lives forever. I haven't met Patrick yet. Well, except for that one time, just briefly, when his wet blanket of a son called the cops. But as I was being dragged past my hero out of his kitchen at 2:30 AM, our eyes met, and in that moment we shared something truly special. My life hasn't been the same since. I think these celebrities' stories will inspire you, too, to follow your dreams of tracking down your idols.

Thanks to this book, I know when I get out I will tirelessly continue my efforts to meet Patrick. And I know that I won't be let down when I finally do. In fact, I know it will be nothing short of Atlantean.

6

Love and Sex

YES, PLEASE

THE JOY OF SEX was an illustrated sex manual that came out in 1972 by author Alex Comfort. (That last name was *very* fitting.) I found a copy of it at home as a young boy and found it rather amusing. Many people did. It was a *New York Times* bestseller and spent over seventy weeks toward the top. It doesn't take a genius to know why the book did well—and continues to do well. Sex sells . . . and so do relationship advice books, sex guides, love stories, and romance novels. If you don't believe me, ask any Jackie Collins or Danielle Steel reader. And remember Madonna's book *Sex?* Probably not, but the book made a lot of waves when it came out and sold a ton in its first week. This chapter is nothing like that Madonna book that included Vanilla Ice for absolutely no reason. This section focuses on two different four-letter words, love and, um, well let's just say what happens between the sheets or in the backseat. While it's a section that guides us toward fake books about love and sex, it hits on some very real issues and advice, notably on self-love, relationships, and a healthy sex life. Go ahead. We'll wait here while you slip into something more comfortable.

BRONSON ARROYO is a former All-Star Major League Baseball pitcher who won a World Series Championship with the Boston Red Sox in 2004 (reversing "the curse"). In his career, during which he also played for the Pittsburgh Pirates, Arizona Diamondbacks, and Cincinnati Reds, he put together a 148–137 record and received a Gold Glove Award. He is also a skilled musician.

Foreword to Richard Hurt's
The Old High Hard One

By Bronson Arroyo

GET ASKED REGULARLY to weigh in on all things baseball. Maybe too many people have my cell phone number, but I'm more than happy to share an opinion on the sport that has been my life for, well, my whole life. Less often (but more than you'd think), I get to talk music. Singing, guitar, Pearl Jam . . . these are as much a part of my life as the bat and ball.

Never before have I been asked to write about love. Richard Hurt's new book, *The Old High Hard One*, is a page-turner for sure and has me considering what I know about lasting love and relationships that work.

Richard and I have been friends since my Red Sox days and he knows the importance I place on the relationships in my life. The tongue-in-cheek "old high hard one" is a baseball metaphor we've been tossing back and forth for years and can refer both to a two-strike knock-you-down inside pitch and a fully erect phallus. So when this book finally came to fruition, he knew that would be the title and that I would have a chance to weigh in.

Richard's expertise in the psychology of relationships, particularly those that knock the shit out of you, and his profound insight into how a couple's sexual bond influences their ultimate success or failure have been lively topics of debate for us over the years. That's not really a surprise, since we disagree on most of our opinions—and always have. But he's a brilliant and fascinating man, and you're more likely to live in the world that the following pages describe than mine. But before you get to what Richard says, here's what I think—and if any of what he says sounds too tough for you, well, just know there's another approach.

Don't get me wrong, I agree with Richard that a relationship is work, and you shouldn't think of it in any other way. But there's more than one way to work. Would you expect to go anywhere over two hundred times a year and not get bored? Of course not! With time, you'd start to notice the imperfections in the place. In a relationship, bickering, feeling annoyed over the smallest slight, and boredom set in with repetition. Instead of allowing your relation-ship to fall into a daily grind and become just as much drudgery as your nine-to-five, you can aim for the relaxation of happy hour, the unpredictability of the holiday party, the thrill of a year-end bonus check, and the exhilaration of your two-week Hawaiian vacation by following these rules.

First, unlike what Richard says about moving in, you DO NOT have to live with your significant other. I actually strongly advise against it. You can keep it fresh if you don't have to see their messes, makeup, dirty closet, eating habits, and so forth. My preference is to live and love from completely different states. Three to five nights together and you head back out. I know what you're thinking, but this is not a ploy to get more action from someone else. (We'll talk about that in a bit.) In fact, it's guaranteed to keep the action coming from your significant other. Absence makes the heart and the nether regions grow fonder. If you do live in the same city, make definite date nights, but do not leave yourself open to last-minute plans. Your days off are your days off—no negotiation once the schedule is set. Everything in life is more enjoyable when it's done in moderation, and your relationship and sex life are no different. Use a fine wine, your favorite rock show, or a great vacation as your guide for managing your relationship. Any of the best things experienced too often will lose their shine.

Want kids? Ignore that impulse. Richard may think they're blessings. The truth is, the world is full of humans and you are programmed to want to pass on your own DNA. But for what, really? If you want to explore your own happiness in adulthood, do not take on a second life's work of being a parent.

Next, make rules and stick to them. Richard recommends stopping contact with all exes once you're in a serious relationship. But I say, keep your friends and ex-girlfriends as close to you as makes you comfortable. What if your woman wants an ex out of your life? That's not up to her. Nor is it up to you who stays close to her. Inside of the relationship, everything must be even, so make sure you're willing to extend as much latitude as you'd like to take. As I mentioned before, staying apart doesn't necessarily mean being promiscuous—*unless* that's what you want. Richard has an unfortunate attachment to those old, stale ideas about monogamy, but take it from me, all sorts of arrangements are OK as long as you're open and honest from the start about who is going to do what, when, and with whom. Once you've laid the ground rules, there's no negotiation, so think carefully about the kind of sex life you truly want before you start, and find a partner who wants the same things you do. If you mistakenly believe that there are no women with your sex goals, you're wrong. But you have to be a worthy mate of those goals as well, so if you're having trouble finding her, take a look at yourself first.

Finally, and most important, when you do have sex, make the most of it. An orgasm is a free ticket to crack-cocaine land for your brain—take advantage of it! Experiment, keep it fresh, enjoy each other before you head back to your own house for some well-earned alone time.

It starts with work and ends with sex, and on these two points, Richard and I have always found common ground. The middle . . . well, that's up to Richard and you for the rest of this book. Happy reading!

INARA GEORGE is a singer-songwriter and musician, one half of the Bird and the Bee (a collaboration with Grammy-winning producer, singer, and instrumentalist Greg Kurstin) and a member of the Living Sisters.

Foreword to Aurora Charming's *The Birds and the Bees: When Prince Charming Discovered Cinderella's Clitoris, Not Her Slipper*

By Inara George

WHEN I WAS A GIRL I used to practice kissing by draping a wet wash-cloth over the side of the bathtub, and then kiss the rim of the tub where I had laid the cloth. I have no idea why I thought that this technique would help give me a leg up in the kissing department. It was just something wet and I guess I figured that would have to do. I mean, how do any of us figure out this stuff? I suppose it's a lot of trial and error. But who are our role models and teachers? Our parents? Are we all doomed to unconsciously recreate the relation-ships we grew up around? My father died when I was five, and my mother never remarried. Maybe that's why I didn't kiss a boy until I was sixteen. I just didn't know how it was done. It scared the shit out of me, and he didn't understand why I kept saying I needed a damp cloth.

Our friends certainly affect our romantic styles. We schemed and strategized to get the coolest, most unavailable guys, even if someone wonderful but dorky was into us. Oh, Kevin Scott. He was the sweet-est guy in the world and not even bad looking. He drove a winding road all the way up to my house just to take me on a date, but I dropped him the second a friend asked if I liked "that nerd." I said no, and never spoke to Kevin again. You can go ahead and judge me, but I'm already remorseful, so what will that help? My whole point is

I didn't know what I was doing back then. If anything, I'm the one that missed out. Is it weird that I'm still sad about this?

Anyway, I don't want to get off track. I didn't know how to do romance, and I didn't know anything about sex, either. Who is really telling us what we need to know before we get tangled up in that? Sex is great. I love sex! Two thumbs up! But why didn't anyone give me a real nuts-and-bolts rundown? (Sex education in school is hardly sufficient, but that's a whole other subject.) My friends didn't know what they were talking about, and I really wasn't prepared to hear about it from my mother.

Now that I'm a mother myself, I realize I had a teacher after all, one I didn't notice was affecting me as I made my way through the minefield of sex and love: princesses! Oh dear God, princesses, fairy tales, and their insidious little messages. And these stories have lodged in our collective minds for centuries. They are beautiful tales, yes, but they got problems! There's Ariel, who gives up her voice just to get on a boat with Eric. Sleeping Beauty finds her greatest love while she's unconscious. Belle's like, "I love reading—oh, and being seduced by a literal monster!" Snow White spends her days doing chores for seven grumbling little dudes. I mean, no wonder I dumped Kevin, amirite?

But there's an even subtler thing that unites those dreamy princesses. They meet a man, fall in love with him almost instantaneously, and *then get married about a week or so later.* We never learn how they dealt with the guys' issues, or learned to talk about feelings, or figured out how to put what part where (can you imagine learning about it from a talking teapot?).

At long last, Aurora Charming has provided an antidote for what ails these stories. *The Birds and the Bees: When Prince Charming Found Cinderella's Clitoris, Not Her Slipper* is funny, fascinating, and should be required reading for all young women and men on the cusp of their romantic journeys. Charming tells the other half of those age-old stories, and in the process, she's rewritten these tales into ones that we can relate to. The Prince's discovery of Cinderella's clitoris was so poignant it brought tears to my eyes. Ariel's intrepid search for her larynx filled me with pride and confidence. And that's just the first two chapters! As a princess herself, Aurora has a unique perspective and deep connections with these ladies, and she takes readers through just what happened after the wedding ended and the credits rolled.

While our culture swings back and forth on its pendulum from conservative to progressive and back again, Charming slices through all the nonsense with simple, useful information, arming her readers with enough knowledge to respect themselves and the ones they love. I was touched and flattered when she reached out to me to ask if I'd be the first to read *The Birds and the Bees*, having been inspired by my song "Would You Be My Fucking Boyfriend." I so wish I had this book during my teenage years! I feel lucky knowing my daughter will have it during hers.

JEFFREY REDDICK is a screenwriter, director, author, and the creator of the Final Destination film franchise.

Foreword to Loosen Mirespect's
Final Penetration: A Novel

By Jeffrey Reddick

WHEN I WAS FIRST ASKED to write the foreword for *Final Penetration*, I was torn. From the title, I was expecting a soapy, tawdry, *Fifty Shades of Grey*–style romance-porn, filled with heaving bosoms and glistening man chests. But there's no sap in this book. No insipid romance.

Final Penetration is an amazing, pulsing, throbbing, life-affirming tome about how sexual innuendo helps a boy grow into a man.

People think sexual innuendos are nothing more than juvenile jokes where a man brags about his big rooster or a woman coos about her moist cat. But as the brilliant author, Loosen Mirespect, showcases in his fascinating debut novel, they can be so much more.

They can change someone's entire world.

Before I get into the book itself, many will guess that Loosen Mirespect is actually the writer's pen name. I met him at a horror convention, and we bonded over the fact that projects involving horror or sex don't get the respect they deserve. I was initially hesitant to write about a nonhorror book involving sex because I was worried what people would think. But Loosen pointed out I was falling into the same repressive mindset I was complaining about. So, I decided to throw caution to the wind and dive balls deep into his magnum opus.

Final Penetration is a steamy yet heartfelt book that unzips the secret world of sexual innuendo. This coming-of-age tale thrusts readers deep into the recesses of the mind of fifteen-year-old Willie Doyle, who dreams of nothing more than writing dirty jokes. But his wet dreams are in danger of being blocked by his dominant father, who spends more time spanking Willie than showering him with love, and a mother more concerned with tilling her own garden than tending to her son.

Willie is a fascinating creation. As he grows from a boy to a strapping young man, he exhibits the hard exterior typical of a early manhood, but starts to withdraw from every conquest that comes his way. For Willie has a softer side that longs to be ploughed in order for the tender flowers containng his dreams to take root. How will he ever loosen up enough to welcome the man inside him?

Salvation comes in the form of Misty Rains, a perky young gypsy who pops in to Willie's life at eighteen. Misty pushes through his defenses and enters his inner sanctum. With Misty guiding him with a gentle but firm touch, Willie truly rises. His creative juices begin to boil, and Willie's true talent can no longer be hidden. Even as the challenges mount, Willie beats off his inner demons and breaks through every dam until he eventually unleashes a torrent of brilliance that drenches the writing world. But more than his incredible literary success, Willie finds new (double) meaning in his life.

True to its title, this book will penetrate you in surprising ways. From its scintillating characters and prickly humor to the pillow-biting suspense and titillating insight, reading *Final Penetration* is a sensory orgy that will leave you breathless and ready for a second round the minute you've finished it off.

Foreword to Prof. Boobsen Plainview's
Nip-Slips: An Illustrated History

Fore(skin)word by Mr. Skin

B EHOLD THE NIP-SLIP—the utmost peak (and peek) example of accidental nudity in the entire Skintheon of Surreptitious Sexposures of
Female Flesh!

Think about it. Hard. Does any other category of fleetingly
glimpsed body bits compare, thrill-wise, to the unintended baring of
a boob-bud, the sudden surfacing of knocker-nozzle, or a momentary
gander at the yob-knob of an otherwise udderly concealed mammary gland?

No way, from cups double-D to triple-A.

In fact, in the realm of happenstance hotness, the nip-slip handily
beats off all other comers—from the thigh-spy to the cheek-peek to
the crack-attack to even the rare (whether hairy or bare) gash-flash.

What is it about a spilled milk-bag that makes our mouths water
so? Why does all of humanity go so skinstantly gaga over a mere hint
of ta-ta tip? What makes the down-blouse or button-busting or by-
any-other-means top-flopping pop-out of a jug-spout so uniquely
skintillating?

The breast is best and that's all there is t(w)o (t)it!

Thus, it was an honor to be contacted by Professor Plainview to
pen the opening to this compendium on surprise looks at rack-rooks
through the ages.

The professor is a man of letters, specializing in the hooter mishaps
of historical figures. Prepare to be enlightened (and elongated) by his

educated analyses of historical skincidents, such as when Cleopatra's asp tore her toga at tit level or when Marie Antoinette bent before the guillotine blade and her gown flopped down far enough to turn the peasants' jeers to pleasant cheers.

I swell as well—with pride—over the fact that Professor Plainview consulted with me on more modern marvels of mammary manifestations in the realm of movie and TV starlets.

Now, since I am known as the world's foremost authority on celebrity nudity, you might think I'm especially well (per)versed in the area of famous fun-pillows that have bounced askew and, gloriously, into rapid view. On that front, you'd be erect. I mean, correct. (OK, you know I actually mean both.) And I would like to take this opportunity to correct a common misapprehension on what we talk about when we talk about nip-slips.

To be sure, we're not dealing with a "wardrobe malfunction" like when Janet Jackson forward-passed her half-a-rack at the 2004 Super Bowl or a comically preplanned whipping out of an upper-deck whoopee cushion akin to Amy Schumer's right-side boomer in the 2017 movie *Snatched*.

No. As much as I bow down (and bone up) to those two titanic displays of Hollywood hooter heat, they lack the specific serendipitous charms of a genuinely unexpected appearance of chest-crest. A true nip-slip has to come out of nowhere and deliver everything.

I initially came across the phenomenon by way of the boob tube. Back in the 1970s, no tele-*vision* extended more antennae than Farrah Fawcett on *Charlie's Angels*. Also bare in mind—pun, as always, intended—that while Farrah headlined the jiggle-heavy ABC hit about three undercover female agents who famously never sported undergarments, she also racked up the highest poster sales of all time when she was photographed brandishing a broad smile, a luminous heap of blond locks, and a skintight swimsuit that showcased her eyepopping, pants-dropping pair of poke-tastic pencil erasers.

Imagine, then, how high young Mr. Skin's personal Nielsen ratings skyrocketed on October 20, 1976, when the *Charlie's Angels* episode "Angels in Chains" featured Farrah and the gals pretending to be wanton women behind bars. While making a break for freedom, the series' leading lust-bomb bends forward so that her work-shirt unfurls and—bam!—there it is: Farrah's naked right Fawcett. I'm still dripping over it!

So, indeed, a true nip-slip combines the epidermal with the ephemeral.

Bouncing from the '70s to the '00s, consider Jennifer Love Hewitt in the 2002 Jackie Chan action-comedy *The Tuxedo*. One-hour, one-minute in, the all-grown-up—and out—*Party of Five* star dunks her famous party of two in a pool and we get a fast blast of Jennifer Love's right-side Hugeness (and never let it be said that Mr. Skin isn't an upstanding supporter of women's rights—and lefts!).

And that's just unzipping the surface of this rich topographical topic. What follows, now, in *Nip-Slips: An Illustrated History* is a Professor Plainview's bumper crop of dairy-doorbells, casaba-crowns, and bazoom-protrusions dating back to coconut-centric cave drawings all the way up to today's headline makers inadvertently treating us to peeks at their torso-shakers.

This book lays bare the simple fact that whether it's Bonnie Parker going semi-starkers in the back of her shot-up Ford or Jackie O unknowingly showing her Jackie T, any woman who slips nip—any time, anywhere—is a superstar!

JAMES ADAM SHELLEY is the lead guitarist and banjoist for the band American Authors. Their songs include "Believer" and "Best Day of My Life."

Foreword to Sarah Linanman's *Where in the World Do I Find Love?: A Journey on Seven Continents*

By James Adam Shelley

I MET SARAH ABOUT EIGHT YEARS AGO on a cold, snowy February night, in a small bar about an hour north of Busan, South Korea—just two foreigners sitting alone at the bar late on a Sunday. I don't even know how the conversation started, but we got to talking, maybe out of loneliness, or maybe just because it had been a while since either of us had spoken English with a native speaker. Sarah motioned to a stocky middle-aged Korean man in a suit sitting at a table with other men his age and explained that she'd moved in with him a few weeks earlier. I remember being very curious about her relationship. Now, I don't personally care who dates whom. But it was interesting to see a white girl from Ontario, Canada, who did not speak Korean, dating a Korean man who she said could only speak a few words of English. She seemed to be such a wild card and a true adventurer. We hugged when we parted ways that night, but I sort of assumed I wouldn't see her again—just a chance encounter in a far-off place.

About a year later, though, I got a message from her. For those of you who have picked up Sarah's book and have no idea who I am, I play in a rock band. I am pretty easy to find because our tour schedule is online, and really anyone who cares to look can see where we will be. She saw I was going to be playing a show in Paris, France, and was asking to come hang. Of course I got her two free tickets. This time she showed up with a dark-haired Frenchman named Andi who was very funny, even if he seemed a little crazy. He kept putting on a bad American accent to rib me, and even tried to convince an English girl he was a surfer from California. After the show, we went to a club near Revolution and partied all night with him and his friends.

Over the next few years, I met Sarah all over the world, from Germany to South Africa to Japan. I even met her in her hometown just outside Toronto when she moved back because she ran out of money. She was dating a local journalist; he struck me as a very intense guy. We most recently met up in Buenos Aires, Argentina, after I spent three weeks climbing a mountain called Aconcagua. It was usually the same situation; Sarah would show up with some local person hanging on her arm and following her every move. But sometimes we'd find time to sit alone, and we would talk for hours and hours about love and what it meant to us, drinking and smoking at some café somewhere in the world.

In Buenos Aires, sitting at another small café, I felt like I was asking her the same questions I'd asked so many times before. Are you lonely? Why are you doing this? Have you just not found "the one" to love? I was always so curious why she would change countries and men every few months. I said she was always so good at pretending at love.

She'd always respond, "I have truly loved every man I have been with, in my own different way. How do you know what true love is if you haven't experienced lots of different kinds of love? Have you ever fallen in love with someone who doesn't speak the same language as you, but you can't resist their energy? Have you ever spent weeks with a person, not talking about stuff that doesn't matter, but just feeling their presence as you drink wine or walk the streets?" She'd sip her drink and continue with the same argument. "There are billions of people in the world. How can you tell if the culture of love in America is best suited for you if you have never loved someone from Turkey? Your version is like only ever eating at one restaurant and saying they definitely serve your favorite food. How could you know? How could you choose?"

"Well," I'd say, "by that argument you will have to sleep with every man on earth to find the perfect one for you." We'd both laugh. "In your version of love, the search is never ending. How can you build long-term love, which is so different from your usual three-month fling?"

And Sarah would tell me, "I'm going to live to 101 years old. When I'm 60, maybe I will find the culture that represents love the best to me. And for now, I want to find every different version of love and experience everything they have to offer. To learn a new culture, you have to eat like the people, sleep like the people, and have sex like the people. One day I will have enough experience to know which life and which love suits me best. And I will take that life and keep living it to the fullest."

I never fully understood why Sarah was the way she was, but I loved the idea of someone traveling the world to find love. Maybe she would find her best version of love in French culture or Argentinian culture or Japanese culture. Maybe she would eventually go back home and find it in Canadian culture. But she had to know for sure. And I admired her courage.

I wasn't surprised when Sarah told me she was writing a book. But I was surprised when she asked me to write this foreword for her. Maybe it was because I was a man who met her on this journey but watched as an outsider. I have been in a relationship for a long time, so I never fully understood her journey to find love. Still, I have a lot of respect for Sarah. As a musician and a dream chaser, I have a hard time relating to most people, regardless of which culture they are from; I relate most to other dream chasers. And Sarah is definitely chasing her own particular dream.

Who knows? Maybe she's right and everyone in their twenties and thirties should take time to travel the world and learn more about love and relationships. In this book, you will read about Sarah's incredible experiences of love all over the world. She tells us not to just settle when it comes to love; go out and find something that's right for you.

Sarah challenges our concept of love and how we are searching for it. Are we doing everything we could?

I hope Sarah finds the perfect kind of love she is looking for. (I think I should warn you: This book doesn't end with a happily-ever-after.) But even if she's still looking for her match, Sarah seems to have found out a lot about human nature and who we are as people. We are so different, but Sarah's stories show that we are all looking for love in our own way in this big crazy world. Reading it feels just like being next to Sarah in some small café in some far-off place. May Sarah's stories make you feel a little less lonely on your own journey, wherever chasing your dream takes you.

7

Science and Nature

ENJOY THEM BEFORE
THEY'RE GONE

FROM DARWIN'S *On the Origin of Species* to Carson's *Silent Spring*, books about science and nature are some of the best-read and most talked-about tomes—and for good reasons. These books help us to learn about our world and the people and creatures that inhabit it. Don't believe me? Look into Shirley MacLaine's books from the 1980s. Wait, they were about the afterlife. But the example still works, right? Right?? Anyway, science and nature are such a huge deal now (unless you're the head of ExxonMobil), so that's where we're taking you next. This chapter hits on both subjects in such a way that you'll be, among other things, questioning why a boy-band superstar retired to become an emu farmer and pondering what it's like to be the world's first pregnant man. You may even feel compelled to pick your nose. This chapter proves why the old saying "reading is fundamental" is totally true.

Foreword to *The Lure of the Flies*, by author unknown

By Adam West

P LEASE ALLOW ME to make a vague and somewhat absurd association with my years playing the classic Batman. You probably know that, at dusk, thousands of bats fly from their caves to gobble insects. They love flies of all shapes, sizes, and colors. So do fish. And so do fly fishers.

The wet and dry fly fisherman probably has a greater variety of flies in his vest than any bat has ever relished in its hairy little mouth. My own fly-casting pastime began many years ago. I grew up with many rivers and good streams nearby. My earlier years were in Walla Walla, Washington, on a ranch. Walla Walla is a Native American name meaning "many waters." You got it. Two Wallas would mean many. Those Umatilla Indians are clever people.

And they are great fishermen. When I was a young boy, my grandfather and I would watch them spear and net salmon in falls and rapids of the majestic Columbia River. They were not fly fishermen to any extent. Leave that to the white man with his dozens of flies at the ready, flies that many of us tie ourselves in order to imitate nature.

I have never seen a bat come after one of my flies, but many times a fish will. I am not sure whether that is an indicator of the relative intelligence between fish and hungry bats. Out of mere loyalty, I would have to bet the latter are the more intelligent. All of this sounds a bit absurd, but please know this writer has spent much of a long career dealing with absurdities and exaggerations.

Most fishermen exaggerate. It is intrinsic to the art of fly fishing. I will confess that one time, while fishing on the glorious south fork of the Snake River, I cast a beautiful line and reeled in a fine but rather small rainbow trout. Naturally, I released this little guy. Later, over a few beers at the end of the day, I must confess that my fish grew in size rather quickly. I hate to disappoint those of you who learned moral and ethical lessons from the Caped Crusader. I lied.

The fly fisherman has in his arsenal many fascinating fake insects. He has at the ready a Parachute Adams, a San Juan Worm, a Woolly Bugger, Pheasant Tail Nymphs, a Bunny Leech, a Gold-Ribbed Hare's Ear. The creel, the vest, the band of your hat will have wet and dry flies of various sizes if you're a serious fisherman. To well cast a line on a wild river, to know you might even land a fish before the bear on the other side of the water does, to breathe clean air, to watch an eagle get curious, to feel as free as the fish you are after . . . It is good to be optimistic in life, to know that you really do have the most deliciously appealing insect on the end of that arching line. Flies can be delicious.

JONATHAN KNIGHT was born and raised in Boston. After finding great success as a member of New Kids on the Block, he moved with his partner, Harley Knight-Rodriguez, to a farm in Essex, Massachusetts, where there is now not an emu to be found.

Foreword to *Everything You Need to Know About Massachusetts Fish and Wildlife Regulations*, by Will D. Beest

By Jonathan Knight

As one-fifth of the 1980s boy band New Kids on the Block, I realize you would probably expect to find my foreword in a book about rat-tails or spandex, not one about regional wildlife regulations. But what you may not know about me is that, in addition to being a New Kid, I am also a former emu farmer.

Because of this, no one can attest to the importance of *Everything You Need to Know About Massachusetts Fish and Wildlife Regulations* better than I can. Is it the most boring book you'll ever read? Well, probably yes. But if you're an emu farmer, trust me—you need to read this book.

When the New Kids broke up in 1994, I was twenty-five. I very quickly realized that retiring to a life of leisure would drive both myself and everyone around me insane. One morning—OK, it was afternoon, but I had just woken up—as I gazed out at my twenty-acre farm in Essex, Massachusetts, it was suddenly so obvious to me what I should do with the rest of my life: raise emus!

If you are not familiar with what an emu looks like, go google it right now.

Are you back?

Yes, those are the beautiful faces to which I wanted to dedicate the next several decades of my life. But, in context, it made sense—emus were the next logical addition to my existing collection of llamas, Texas longhorn cattle, and z-donks (a cross between a zebra and a donkey).

I went running back into the house to share my stroke of genius with my mom, who was living with me at the time.

"Jon," she confirmed, "that's *genius!*"

I should add here that, at the time, my mother was the queen of (unsuccessful) get-rich-quick schemes. It just so happened that she had recently caught wind that emu mania was about to sweep through America, so she was 100 percent positive a flock of emus would be a lucrative investment. What could go wrong?

A few months later, a trailer containing three pairs of (very expensive) mated emus pulled up to my gate. These prize birds were guaranteed to provide me with all the offspring I would need to start building my emu empire.

The truck driver asked me where he should put the emus. *Hmmm*, I hadn't thought that far ahead. I did a quick survey of my property, and the unused tennis court caught my eye. Perfect! It would make a natural emu habitat. The only thing that would make a personal tennis court more of a status symbol than it already was is a tennis court full of little emus. Okay, big emus, because, let me tell you, emus are some large birds.

Once the emus were in their tennis court, I had my next stroke of genius. Who better to supervise the construction of the emu habitat than me? Sure, I had no experience in construction at all, but it couldn't be too difficult.

Turns out, I loved supervising. So much that I decided to throw myself into the mix so that I could *really* be at one with the emu habitat. The pneumatic nail gun looked like it would be a great foray into power tools, so I figured I'd start with that. About an hour later, I found myself in the emergency room with a board attached to my hand.

The habitat got finished anyway, and it seemed like it would be smooth sailing from there. Thanks to an incubator the size of a refrigerator that I set up in my laundry room, those bad boys multiplied like gremlins, only they were way cuter!

Realizing I was well on my way to making a fortune, I did what any savvy investor would do: I insured my flock with the only company that would insure them, Lloyd's of London. A year later, everything was still going well, and I realized, "Boy, this insurance is really expensive," so I canceled it. Even more savvy! I was a financially conservative investor.

And, then . . . I watched in slack-jawed horror as, one after another, emus started dropping dead on my tennis-court-turned-emu-habitat. A couple of days later, as I was running around in a panicked, futile effort to resuscitate fallen emus and drag their lifeless bodies out of the pen, I saw a trail of forest green vans and pickup trucks coming up the hill to my house.

A man dressed like he was about to go on safari emerged from one van. "Sir," he informed me, "there's been a report of an outbreak of encephalitis on your farm. We're going to have to ask you to shut it down."

For the second time in my life, I made professional history—there had never before been an outbreak of emu encephalitis in Massachusetts.

Where my tennis court once stood, today stands a mass emu burial ground. Sometimes I wake up at night with the vision of hundreds of emus being bulldozed into the mass grave I buried them in, convinced that those strange sounds outside are zombie emus coming to get me.

So, do yourself a favor—before you order yourself some emus, read this book.

Best-selling, award-winning children's musician **LAURIE BERKNER** has been a longtime fixture on TV's Nick Jr. and Universal Kids channels, and her 10-chapter series, Laurie Berkner's Song & Story Kitchen, may be heard on Audible. Laurie's original songs, albums, DVDs, music videos, and books leave no doubt: Laurie is the uncrowned queen of children's music and the power behind the progressive "kindie rock" movement.

Foreword to *The Psychology of Chickens*, by the Daughters of the American Chicken Revolution

By Laurie Berkner

CHICKENS. We all love 'em. But do we really *know* them? The Leghorn, the Silkie, the Rhode Island Red: these intriguing and provocative names might say something about a bird's outer appearance—but what about her inner nature?

We as a culture are creating more and more "chick lit" every day to satisfy our desire to better understand these creatures. I stop on the street almost daily to chat with people about our obsession with really seeing things from the hen's point of view. We admit to hoarding piles of magazines like *KFC Is Not My Colonel* and *It's a Bird's Life*. We spend countless hours poring over it all, imagining a simpler time when happily clucking together and learning the art of head-bobbing would be our only responsibilities.

I would be remiss, of course, if I didn't mention the resources that are out there already. We have the self-proclaimed prophet Chicken Little, the model of industriousness the Little Red Hen, and the eponymous "chicken dance" that makes people feel excited about singing "bawk bawk bawk bawk" in unison and flapping their arms like wings (which of course originated from mimicking the difficulty chickens themselves have when trying to *actually* fly).

166

Somehow, even with all of this, we have remained in the dark as to the *true* reason why the chicken crossed the road.

While singers and songwriters have been crowing about chickens since songwriting began, with classics like "There Ain't Nobody Here but Us Chickens" by Louis Jordan (also performed by James Brown, B. B. King, and the Muppets), "Eye of the Chicken" by the Butthole Surfers, and even "Know Your Chicken" by Cibo Matto, we all understand that it takes a true chicken authority to really know them.

Therefore, I was truly honored when the Daughters of the American Chicken Revolution asked me to write this foreword to their *The Psychology of Chickens*. I believe they were inspired because of my song "I Know a Chicken." And as you can tell from the lyrics, it reflects my deep understanding and instinctive connection to these birds.

"I know a chicken, and she laid an egg. I know a chicken, and she laid an egg. Oh my goodness, it's a shaky egg."

Do yourself a favor and read this fantastic guide to understanding fowl psychology. Discover how we are all connected to these small, feathered, sometimes nasty, and yet still noble creatures that we all want to know. Then go out and cross the road to the chicken's side. You'll find that once you get there, having read this book, you too will be able to sing "I Know A Chicken"—and really mean it.

Foreword to *A Brief History of the Chewing Patterns of the Reticulated Giraffe*, by P. Forsythe Wellington

By Steve Hofstetter

DEAR READER! I am honored to have been chosen to write the foreword to P. Forsythe Wellington's *A Brief History of the Chewing Patterns of the Reticulated Giraffe*. As I am sure you already know, Mr. Wellington is the foremost expert on the reticulated giraffe, and, most important, its chewing patterns. But something you might not know is that Mr. Wellington is also a hell of a cardplayer!

Funny story: Forsie and I were at a cash game in Hong Kong. I was showing a pair of sevens and . . . fuck, I can't do this.

I've never met P. Forsythe Wellington. I don't give a shit about giraffes. The truth is, when I signed the contract to write this stupid thing, I thought I was agreeing to be a backup dancer for Reel Big Fish.

Now that I think about it, they don't have backup dancers. I was really, really high.

The chewing patterns of reticulated giraffes? They eat, no one cares. Boom, end of book, now go read Harry Potter. Who chooses to be called "P" instead of their real name? How bad do you think his real name is? It's Priscilla, isn't it? Maybe Penelope. Oh! Maybe it's Penelope, but it's pronounced "Peen-a-lope."

At least no one I know is going to see this.

Well, read the damned book. Or don't. I don't care. I fulfilled my contract and never have to think about giraffes again. I tried reading it myself. Couldn't get through the first chapter. This book is as bad as being named Peenalope. The most interesting part of this process for me was googling if the word is spelled "forward" or "foreword."

I do have one piece of advice: Don't ever do cocaine off a book contract.

This check better clear.

JEFF PEARLMAN is the *New York Times* bestselling author of seven books, a columnist for the *Athletic*, and host of the weekly podcast *Two Writers Slinging Yang*. Visit him at jeffpearlman.com.

Foreword to Dr. Robert Mochahu's *Boogers That Taste like Cheese: A Rigorous Scientific Inquiry*

By Jeff Pearlman

WHEN MY ESTEEMED COLLEAGUE, Dr. Robert Mochahu of the Garry Templeton Institute of Finite Finger Gestures, first asked whether I would write a foreword for this magnificent, compassionate, and historically significant book, I was both honored and bewildered.

Honored, because Dr. Mochahu is one of the leaders of his field.

Bewildered, because *Boogers That Taste like Cheese* struck me as an odd title for an academic work. And though we are colleagues at the Templeton Institute, my expertise on finite finger gestures has revolved around their application in the world of sports; as Dr. Mochahu is a psychologist, our fields of inquiry seldom overlap.

With precedent as my guide, I presumed the five words served as a global metaphor. Perhaps "boogers" symbolized the hardened shell we all use to guard others from seeing our true selves. Perhaps "cheese" was the inner desire of our suppressed id melting away. In those contexts, I considered this to be (potentially) among the world's key post–B. F. Skinner psychological analyses.

Yet when I ran my theory by Dr. Mochahu, he shook his head and decisively grunted, "No."

Then came words I will never forget: "The book," he pronounced, "is about boogers that taste like cheese."

Dr. Mochahu's brilliance knows no bounds.

Over the course of the 784 pages that follow, my friend and lifelong mentor will take you on a riveting journey that incorporates boogers, cheese, and how boogers taste like cheese.

It all dates back to an otherwise forgettable day in the spring of 1957, when Dr. Mochahu, then but a boy of four growing up in the mountains of Kissimmee, Florida, felt the urge to extend his right index finger up his left nostril. He jarred loose a pea-sized booger, brought it toward his tongue, then noted to his older brother Gerald that the taste reminded him of the finest of Bries.

"So," Gerald said, "you picked a booger that tastes like cheese?"

"Yes," replied young Robert. "I picked a booger that tastes like cheese."

Few could have predicted the literary brilliance that, six decades later, would follow. This astonishing work, blending never-before-published research and Dr. Mochahu's wise insights into human nature, will have far-reaching implications across the arts and sciences. Indeed, psychologists, biologists, gastronomes, and even everyday readers will find much to reflect on in these pages.

To be honest, I never before thought boogers tasted like cheese. My own boogers tend to have a cranberry-like tang that my wife, Catherine, sometimes confuses for marmalade. Hers, on the other hand, are crisp and refreshing, much akin to a wedge of iceberg lettuce with a dollop of Thousand Island. Why, I was seven the first time I tasted the boogers of another's nasal cavity. My Aunt Rose, ninety-eight and prepared to depart this world, was lying on a hospital bed, wrinkled, weathered, battered from a life of hardship. She called me—her favorite of seventeen nephews—to her side, gently kissed my forehead and whispered into my ear, "Dear Jeffrey, before I go, please try my boogers."

I did as I was told, and as my quivering left pinky entered her slim nostril, love reigned. I gently removed a small, crusty, slightly bloody booger and tasted it. Far from delicious, the unfamiliar spiciness sent a jolt through my core.

"Cumin," Aunt Rose sighed, "and tarragon."

With that, she was gone. Eternal sleep had beckoned.

So, yes, based upon my own personal history, Dr. Mochahu's controversial theory—that boogers taste like cheese—caused quite the internal stir.

Recently, he invited me to his private home office, where alongside the world's fifth-largest collection of precolonial armpit grease, he keeps a large wooden box labeled, simply, B.T.T.L.C. After opening three locks and typing in a twelve-digit passcode, Dr. Mochahu pulled back the lid and said, "Behold."

Indeed, it was a vision unlike any I had ever witnessed. Boogers glued to boogers glued to more boogers. Some were green. Some were yellow. Some were green and yellow. It smelled of honey, lemon, and righteousness.

Dr. Mochahu explained how the boogers—carefully extracted over twenty-five years—belonged to international superstars ranging from Bob Tewksbury and Tommy Shaw to Emmanuel Lewis and three of the twelve Menudo members.

"Try some?" he said.

At the risk of letting down millions of readers, I will not reveal here whether the boogers did, in fact, taste like cheese. But I will say, Dr. Mochahu is rarely wrong. Readers, it is my distinct pleasure to introduce you to this thought-provoking, life-changing work.

LERA LYNN is a Nashville-based singer-songwriter specializing in original post-Americana music.

Foreword to Dr. Adelicia Wolfe's *The Life and Love of Dr. Viktor Wolfe: Innovator, Activist, Husband, Father, Mother*

By Lera Lynn

D<small>R. V</small>IKTOR W<small>OLFE</small> was a modern-day hero. He was a martyr and a visionary. He was a husband and—as he'd say, most important—he was a father.

When his wife and counterpart in breakthrough medical science, Dr. Adelicia Wolfe, suffered her fifth failed pregnancy, he asked one simple question: "Why can't I carry our child?"

The couple began work on one of the most radical pursuits in the history of medical science, and what ensued over the next twenty-five years would surprise even them. From A-list celebrities to human rights activists, ballsy politicians, and a whole gang of tireless pro bono lawyers, the response from supporters was shocking. The unsolicited financial support they received was astounding. Those twenty-five years were countless hours of painstaking work, relentless scrutiny and criticism, media cyclones, dodged assassination attempts, incarcerations, and eventual imperative reclusion.

Despite the extreme controversy, the political and social uproar, and his wrongful imprisonment, Dr. Viktor Wolfe, by way of his own medical technology, became the first man to successfully carry and deliver a child to full term. That child was me.

This is the story of nothing impossible, of burning red tape, smearing party lines, and of human rights on steroids. This is the story of the twenty-five-year fight that led only recently to the legalization of male pregnancy—one of the biggest breakthroughs of our time.

This is also the story of unfathomable *love* and unrelenting bravery told by the only person truly qualified to tell it: my mother, Dr. Adelicia Wolfe. This amazing woman was by his side every day, until his death did them part. This is *her* story of that exceptional pregnancy, day by day. Dr. Wolfe weaves through her story the mundane yet miraculous details of their pregnancy, the full story of which has never before been told. You are with them through the fear and the pain, the uncertainty and meltdowns, the mood swings and cravings, the miracle and the victory. (You'll be as surprised and touched as I was to read how my stalwart father overcame severe morning sickness.) Perhaps the most compelling story here is of their discovery of a love deeper than ever imagined as they became the first of our *species* to embark upon such a journey. For expectant parents of any gender, may this book be an inspiring, guiding light on your own pregnancy journey.

At thirty years old, I said goodbye to my father. I am thrilled to pay tribute to his exceptional life, and his undying love. I wish he were able to see how all of his sacrifice and unfathomably hard work would come to fruition and change the lives of so many. And he would be thrilled to know that my husband is expecting our first child any day now!

JEREMY KAPLAN is editor in chief of Digital Trends, one of the world's largest technology publishers, and responsible for keeping the site awesome. Before joining DT, he was science and technology editor at FoxNews.com and spent over a dozen years at tech magazine publisher Ziff Davis testing products and reporting on trends as the technology industry exploded. He still finds it all fascinating to watch.

Foreword to Sheila Van Hoovens's Driven: One Man's Quest to Perfect the Flying Car

By Jeremy Kaplan

NATHAN FLINGER must have really loved *The Jetsons*. How else to explain a lifetime pursuit of the flying car, an ambition that dozens had tried—and failed at—before him? A pursuit the Federal Aviation Administration warned him to end—and for which it fined him repeatedly? A passion that landed him in prison for six months? A dream turned nightmare that ultimately consumed and destroyed him—and dented society as little as a pebble against a 747 wing?

It's this single-minded obsession Sheila Van Hoovens seeks to explore within these pages. When Sheila, a friend and fellow technology journalist, told me she was researching Nathan Flinger, I couldn't have been more amazed. It's rare to find someone else interested in the man's obscure story; until now, he's been at best a bizarre footnote in history. But the life story of this little-known inventor takes more turns than an Indy car. And like those drivers, his crash feels inevitable.

We first meet a young Flinger growing up in a wealthy suburb of Detroit. Eventually, his family moves to California, where he becomes a part of the drag racing scene. In the course of her research, Van Hoovens uncovered unexpected connections between the racing and underworld zine scenes—a connection that proves pivotal in *Driven*. While killing time before a race that would claim the life of his best friend, Flinger picked up a tiny California monthly called *Astro, Where Are You?* It was in these pages that Flinger first met his future. The article in question, a strange modern take on Evelyn Waugh's classic *Brideshead Revisited*, described the downward spiral of a headstrong upstart under the twin influences of drink and a wealthy socialite; absurdly, it takes place within the confines of a flying car. As Van Hoovens describes it, both the article and the accident had an indelible effect on the mind of the young Flinger.

Van Hoovens tirelessly tracked the zine down (only a few hundred were printed), and called it and its author "as dumb as a box of rocks." Flinger fell in love with it, however—and determined that the car must be created.

The story is an apt one, yet Flinger likely didn't see the parallels Van Hoovens is able to draw. Like the protagonist before him, Flinger's life would run out of control even as his dreams took flight.

Van Hoovens takes us on a ride at race car speed through Flinger's personal and professional lives: the off-ramp of his courtship of, marriage to, and disgraceful divorce from a beauty pageant winner. The early head start of winning a Californian funny-bike competition and being able to use the winnings to found his flying car company, Flinger's Wingers. The delays caused by his intellectual limitations as he struggled to make a car light enough to fly. The U-turn of his rampant "borrowing" from the designs of his colleague, and the ensuing complications from the jail time that followed. Like the character that inspired him from the pages of *Astro, Where Are You?*, Flinger was a failure, a truth he sought to avoid (along with debts too monstrous to bear) through long tours of the country and binge drinking. Though at times Flinger acted erratically, Van Hoovens confided in me that she couldn't help but admire his single-minded determination, and that she felt for him when he faltered. Her empathy for Flinger helps us to understand the man in ways his previous chroniclers (few as they are) haven't been able to touch; it's as though she can't wait to introduce us to him in chapter one.

As she traces both rise and fall, Van Hoovens also pushes us to consider the societal implications of single-minded visionaries like Flinger. As children, we are taught that we can accomplish anything, that the world is as boundless as the seas. How does society square that message with an understanding that our passions should perhaps be tempered, the hard edges of our dreams flattened out, lest they turn into nightmares too demanding for our frail minds?

Flinger's collapse could be taken as a warning not to fly too close to the sun, a modern-day Icarus fable discouraging dreamers. Instead, in Van Hoovens's deft hands, Flinger still inspires. Without treasure hunters willing to sail to the edge of the map, without inventors strapping feathered wings to their arms, our world would be small indeed, regardless of success or failure. Shoot for the moon and only make it halfway? You're still halfway to the moon, aren't you?

Nathan Flinger's untimely death—penniless, drunk, and grounded—came before Flinger's Wingers took its first flight. And yet, today, he lives again in these pages. And his invention lives on in a Detroit museum, where it and his tale may hopefully inspire a young generation of dreamers.

Even though it still refuses to fly.

BILL "SPACEMAN" LEE is a former Major League Baseball pitcher who played for the Boston Red Sox (1969–1978) and the Montreal Expos (1979–1982). On November 7, 2008, Lee was inducted into the Red Sox Hall of Fame, as the team's record holder for most games pitched by a left-hander (321) and the third-highest win total (94) by a Red Sox southpaw. On August 23, 2012, at age sixty-five, Lee signed a contract to play with the San Rafael Pacifics of the independent North American League.

Foreword to Vida Blue Azul's *Losing Paluto: The Doomed Quest to Save the Domed Planet*

By Bill Lee

N OT SINCE ALVIN TOFFLER'S *Future Shock* has there been a more gutsy exposé. By now, everyone on Earth has heard of Paluto, the domed planet designed by scientists and economists to run off its own waste. That was the good news. The bad news: nobody actually learned how to deal with waste properly and there were not enough natural supplies to go around! The inhabitants quickly used up their vital resources and began shitting in—excuse me, polluting—their precious water supplies. Hmm . . . sound familiar?

Vida Blue Azul, the Brazilian rain forest advocate (formerly a part-time one-armed logger, but that's another story) moved to Paluto in 2019, before things went south, and invited me to visit—thinking it would be great for me, the Spaceman, a very educated man and also a space traveler, to be the first celebrity to see this brave new world. (Also, I'm the only compatriot who knows what the ankle bracelet is for.) We go way back, me and Vida.

As a survivor of the tragedy, Blue Azul writes a poignant take on how it all went terribly wrong. You'll read more about exactly what happened—Blue Azul gives us chapter after chapter of where we went wrong. But as I see it, the tragedy on Paluto was the result of sheer arrogance, everyone climbing (or one might say clawing) their way to the top of the shit pile. And we could have done something about it, but the networks were all saying the trouble on Paluto was "fake news." The important information coming out of Paluto was trumped by the right-wing negative press. They claimed the reports were coming from "Chicken Little" and the "wrong people" . . . even as the cameraman stepped right into a pile of shit.

The whole problem was that the model for Paluto was based on a false premise. And we've known it for hundreds of years! Thomas Robert Malthus, economist for the East India Company, stated in the 1700s that "goods grow arithmetically and population grows exponentially." Then, economist Adam Smith said, "You got to get as much as you can, as fast as you can, even if it takes two hands." (The problem with *that* was that most of the commoners have their hands tied behind their backs, metaphorically speaking.) The human population always grows faster than resources. Engel and Marx wrote about it a hundred years later in *The Communist Manifesto*. The solution isn't pretty. As Jonathan Swift once wondered, how many calories in a fat Irish kid? (To paraphrase: eat the rich.) . . . At least I think I remember that right.

Which brings us around to 2024, when we found out there was not enough to go around. Vida Blue says all this could have been avoided if we had just learned to pick up our plastic and recycle our BS. We have to change our evil ways (like it said in that Santana song in 1969—same year I was drafted. Hmm . . .). We see the trouble coming. We have to put down our phony idols, our Bibles, and our guns. Vida hopes we learn from Paluto's cautionary tale. For readers of *Operating Manual for Spaceship Earth* and all people interested in saving the planet, this book is here to show why we have to change before another Paluto occurs.

Best regards,

Bill "Earthman" Lee

8

Self Help and Good Advice

BECAUSE YOU NEED SOMEBODY

P RESIDENT RONALD REAGAN once said, "We can't help everyone, but everyone can help someone." It's so true that we could all use a little assist every now and then. (If you saw the Genesis "Land of Confusion" music video, Ronnie certainly did.) Self-help, advice, and how-to books have been fixtures on bestseller lists for years. For example, *How to Win Friends and Influence People* has been in print since 1936. *The 7 Habits of Highly Effective People* has been reissued in so many special new editions that the author has added a new foreword *and* a new afterword. And *The Secret* is a worldwide smash that has sold over thirty million copies and has been translated into fifty languages. So what if the book's "secret" has been disproved? There's an endless supply of sometimes-contradictory advice out there, so if these books work for you, more power to ya (and more money for Tony Robbins!). Anyway, this chapter strives to help you build confidence, hone improv skills, invest well, and so much more. So, draw a warm bath, keep an open mind, and get ready to change your life.

REGINA DECICCO is a playwright and comedian. Currently, Regina is the warm-up comedian on ABC's *The View*. She is also a guest contributor to *The Howard Stern Show* on SiriusXM. She is a regular performer at the world-famous Friars Club and has been a part of the Nantucket Comedy Festival, the Laughing Skull Comedy Festival in Atlanta, Georgia, and Boston's Women in Comedy Festival. Before taking the plunge into stand-up comedy, she spent many years working behind the scenes at *Saturday Night Live*.

Foreword to *I'm Dying Over Here & It's Hilarious: How to Put the FUN in FUNerals!*, by Grandma

By Regina DeCicco

THOUGH IT DIDN'T COME as a surprise, I am honored that my grandmother chose me to write the foreword for her book, *I'm Dying Over Here & It's Hilarious: How to Put the FUN in FUNerals!* All her friends were dying, and each wake was becoming so boring that my grandma started to wish *she* were the one in the casket.

We spent many a sleepless night discussing how she would want things done differently at her memorial, and I urged her to put her thoughts into words. I encouraged her to write this book so grandchildren all over the world could do one last thing to make their grandparents proud.

With the help of this thoughtful guide, Grandma hopes to encourage mourners to turn that frown upside down. Why use that tiny box of tissues for wiping away tears of sadness when you can use them for tears of joy? Forget about the etiquette you've been taught—you can't spell funeral without FUN! This how-to book addresses every myth that surrounds proper behavior during the bereavement process.

Grandma starts with general rules that apply to everyone, so it doesn't matter if the departed was a relative or barely an acquaintance.

Whether you're a pallbearer or a passerby, Grandma knows just what you should do. For example, if the deceased was 102 years old, it's OK to ask the cause of death. The question is rhetorical, and it should break the ice. You want to let everyone there know you are ready to have a good time.

Chapter two speaks directly to the dearly departed's family. You'll find helpful advice for seeing to the estate. Be proactive and ask what will happen to the deceased's belongings, but be specific and helpful. Try shouting out, "I got dibs on everything that's Velcro!"

In chapter seven Grandma addresses the mourners. She really wants the grieving masses to know they are not merely taking up seats, they need to be actively participating. Always be present and appear as though you're taking attendance and then ask, "Is her husband here? I'd like to meet him." Everyone knows if Grandma is 102, Grandpa must've died in like '92, so that will surely elicit a chuckle or guffaw.

If you're a former colleague, then chapter nine is for you. When introducing yourself to family members you haven't met, make sure your relationship with the deceased sounds inappropriate: "Hello, I've been very fortunate, I worked under your grandma. A lot." And don't forget to include an exaggerated wink at the end of your statement. Rest assured, Grandma is looking down on you and she is winking right back.

Let's say you're an enemy of the deceased; don't fret, because Grandma has an idea. Someone just died, so admittedly, you can't just walk into the wake and be an outright jerk. But there *is* a way you can have your cake and eat it, too. Remember, the laughs don't have to stop at the wake; there is fun to be had afterward. When choosing your name for the sign-in book, don't underestimate the power of a classic like "Heywood Jablowme" or "Seymour Butts." Did "Ben Dover" really swing by? He sure did! Try making it a game and involve other attendees, and always be inclusive, not exclusive. The deceased's family will surely appreciate your antics when writing out thank-you cards, especially when they get to "Connie Lingus" and her best friend "Fannie Licker."

So the next time a picture in the obituaries looks familiar, instead of dreading it, you'll be raring to go thanks to Grandma's how-to words of wisdom.*

Enjoy this book and mourn responsibly. Remember: Grandma might be dead, but the last thing she would have wanted is for everyone to be bored to death at her funeral.

---

*Please note, this book is specific to the timely death of an elderly person, though there may be exceptions. This book does not apply to pill overdoses, unless the victim was drinking from an oversized pimp cup or a comically large glass of wine. Do not reference this book if the victim died in a car accident, unless it was a clown car accident and the deceased was a drifter—preferably an unattractive, childless drifter. If the victim was killed petting a shark and you are not sure if this book applies to you, then use this book on yourself, because your sense of humor died years ago. Go directly to chapter five if the victim was the girl who was mean to you in high school.

Foreword to Brittany Brave's *Too Fake to Fail—The Brave Method: How to Use Improv to Win at Life, Love, and Work*

By "Jane Smith," aspiring comedian

WHAT DO COMEDY AND MONEY LAUNDERING have in common? More than you think.

In fact, the two go hand in hand. Like peanut butter and jelly. Hangovers and marathons of *Law and Order: SVU*. Bike rides and yeast infections.

You get the picture.

For decades, I heard people go on and on about how comedy was all about honesty and the constant search for this "truth." (All this along with a slew of other half-baked concepts such as "global warming," "gluten," and "abstinence.") But quickly after deciding to pursue comedy, I learned that this buzz-worthy "truth" . . . is what you make it.

Too Fake to Fail unpacks author, comedian, and generational inspiration Brittany Brave's theories on the hidden value in doing improv. Eight years ago I enrolled in Brave's Improv 101 class as a mandatory requirement during my stint at AA. Never in my wildest detox dreams would I have imagined so many effective, unorthodox ways to exploit each of improv's dynamic tools to get what you want all the time, any time. I'd like to think that today I'm a better woman for it.

I used to think improv was just silly and entertaining, but seasoned comedians know there's much more to discover. When properly practiced, improv is a way to cheat the system. Brave's curriculum, outlined in this book, reveals valuable tactics that can allow people to maintain their vices and prime them to totally best every scenario, all under the seemingly innocent alias of "playing pretend." Indeed, art can truly enhance life, though in this case, it might not keep you from going to jail. (But can you imagine the material from bunking in a penitentiary? I just came up with *at least* four penis jokes. Word play is so fun. I love being witty.)

Take it from me, a student of comedy with no moral compass: Would I have had that seven-year affair with a married man had I not started improv? No way. I was able to travel the Mediterranean on his kid's college fund because I used **"yes-and" thinking**: "**Yes,** I will sleep with you, **and** I do not care that you have a wife."

One of improv's other golden rules is that **there are no mistakes**. Once I opened my eyes to this concept, I became more productive and content. I started to live completely free of remorse or regard for other human beings, both in and out of improv class. What a progressive way to operate as a member of society! Brave's curriculum is rooted in these guilt-proof exercises, and now they are outlined here so you, too, can embrace the ways improv liberates a responsible (read: boring!) conscience.

Shortly after I had finished all thirty-three levels of training, the CEO of my company approached me at our holiday party. For context, I had just drunkenly smashed a festive ice luge in the shape of a reindeer projectile-spewing gallons of Absolut to partygoers. Forgive me for being a bit clumsy when I'm inappropriately intoxicated, but I barreled right through the thing and completely cut off the vodka supply to the rest of my coworkers—forcing them into unbearable levels of sobriety for the rest of the evening. However, I refused to apologize to anyone. Instead, I insisted that it was completely intentional. In fact, I demanded a raise for making such a **confident choice**, and I was able to leave that terrible job when he **gave me the gift** of being fired. Let's give credit for this milestone where credit is due: improv comedy.

Scenes require **character work**. Performers spend a few minutes in the life of another person or profession and learn how to believably wear many hats. That's why, to date, I've delivered thirteen babies. I'm godmother to two of them. Now, I studied liberal arts in college, and I actually failed high school biology. These women had no clue, and the hospital now has me in a regular rotation. I'm not even old enough to be a gynecologist—but **improv makes *anything* possible**!

With improv, as long as you use your imagination, you can have a whole new host of family, friends, and companions to deploy when you most need their support. For example, I invented Snickerdoodle the other day. He is the fat, hairy, and completely nonexistent cat my grandmother gave to me at the tender age of thirteen. Now, imagine he's dead. He has to be, since I just missed my flight to my friend's dream wedding in Reno, Nevada. I created this entire story in minutes, but before you know it, I'm wholly **committed to this narrative**. I had the airline attendant in tears. We swapped our favorite Phil Collins deep cuts, as anyone in deep grief does. I am seconds away from her graciously placing me on another flight because I *clearly* couldn't be punctual in a state of mourning. At some point, the flight attendant starts to surmise that this heartwarming story of my recently deceased cat might be a figment of my imagination (the scientific term for "bullshit"). I panic. I've got to make this wedding. I've got a lot banking on this, and I always do well in Nevada. But suddenly, Sarah from Delta Airlines wants to call my grandmother to make sure my story checks out.

I insist that poor Nana is blind, so she'll have no idea who that fat, hairy feline was. Bless her heart, she was always under the impression that she gifted me with one of her vintage minks. The dear.

See? I both **<u>thought on my feet</u>** *and* made that flight. My friends, however, went through a brutal divorce two short years later. Clearly, some of us commit to a narrative better than others. I thank improv for that, and you soon will, too.

Now, I understand—one wouldn't normally watch a group of grown-ass adults pretend to be Jell-O cups as they frolic around a black box theater and think that particular art form could be influential, or even remotely useful. That's where *Too Fake to Fail* comes in: It's an in-depth survey of the *real* purpose of unscripted comedy. Its exercises are actually a bag of societal tricks that can help us get away with tons of shit and constantly get what we want.

Whether you're new to the art form, or new to burning bridges, Brave will help you cast social responsibility to the wayside, realize your full potential, and maybe even make someone laugh along the way.

On and off stage, readers should remember that **<u>the rule is that there are no rules</u>**. You do not have to follow this book step by step. You always have the option of making it up as you go along.

After all, it's just a **<u>suggestion.</u>**

ALI SPAGNOLA (@alispagnola) is a pop/rock/electro musician, comedian, visual artist, and exceptional high-fiver. She is known for her comedy and music videos, Snapchat stunts, free painting project, and One-Gal Band covers on YouTube. Ali's songs have also appeared on MTV's *Real World* and Oxygen's *Bad Girls Club*.

Foreword to Daffy Duck's *How to Win Influence and Friend People*

By Ali Spagnola

HAVE TO ADMIT, I was quite flattered when I was asked to write the foreword to this book. One of the prominent characters of our time, Daffy Duck, wanted to include me in his newest business venture.

I've been a full-time influencer for over three years now, and I imagine that fact—along with my extensive reading of personal transformation, self-improvement, success, and performance-increasing books—was the reason Daffy found me so fitting for this foreword. Actually, I usually opt for the term "artist" or "creator" over "influencer," but I know Daffy would much more appreciate a title that speaks of power and leverage. So, "influencer" it is.

I began by calling Daffy a prominent character, but he is not so much "prominent" in the "famous" sense but more like the "obtrusive" sense. A book about how to grow on social media would naturally come from such a bold personality. (Some might say "gloryhound," but I will stick with "bold" because I imagine he may skim this.) His tips and tricks, like most people's advice about growing one's online presence, are heavy on the tricks. It's quite a handy guide if you're seeking status yet aiming to hide it under the guise of connectivity and sociability.

Daffy and I both believe success comes from two things; it's just that our two things differ. I believe that success is a combination of hard work and luck. Luck is the most prominent component for me at the moment because I am learning that I don't have control over so many aspects of my career. I now fight to stop my lack of control from discouraging me, and I focus instead on what I can control: the hard work. This shift has been very freeing.

Daffy, on the other hand, asserts it merely takes hard work and social climbing (the latter I would also put under the category of hard work). He represents the classic American dream. If you work your hardest, you can achieve anything you desire. Mr. Duck has worked his hardest on this book. And yet, ironically, this book will probably sell poorly.

I do agree with Daffy that as you're building your online presence and business you should let self-interest be your guide. But Daffy directs you to follow where the algorithm leads. This may mean publishing things that provoke outrage, stooping to the lowest common denominator of toilet humor, or resorting to cute animals to reach as many people as possible. He reveals how the social networks are feedback loops that teach you what "art" to create.

Now, my definition of letting your self-interest be your guide is a bit different. I know I'm not the first person to tell you to follow your passion. Yet I will say it here just the same: Follow your passion. I feel it is especially important in this climate that tells you to read all your comments, create what your users suggest, follow what gets the most views, and so on. Doing this, I have found, is a recipe for bad art, creating things that really don't move you, ending up topless, and a myriad of other things that are unfulfilling. Create what you love. Perhaps you will get lucky and other people will love it, too, but you don't have control over that. Focus on what you can control—the hard work and your own style—and make art that energizes you.

If you take Daffy's advice, you will maybe grow an audience, you will maybe have influence, you will maybe be able to create online for a living, but that is only a maybe. In addition, it will be influence over an audience of awful people you don't truly connect with and you will be creating things you don't truly enjoy.

I have to admit, I'm now quite embarrassed I was asked to write the foreword to this book. Ah, well. At least now you've been warned. With that, here is *How to Win Influence and Friend People.*

KAY HANLEY (@kayhanley) is lead singer for Letters to Cleo. She has written and performed music for film (*Ten Things I Hate About You, Josie and the Pussycats*) and writes/composes music for television (*Doc McStuffins*). She is also Henry Eisenstein's mom.

Foreword to Henry Eisenstein's *Obvious Investing: From Stocks and Bonds to IPOs, It's Just Not That Complicated, Jeez*

By Kay Hanley

O VER THE COURSE OF THE LAST YEAR, fourteen-year-old Henry Eisenstein has developed an astonishing gift for discovering a subject of even nominal interest to him and quickly becoming an expert in that thing.

Eisenstein's latest concern, the stock market, is no different. In this revolutionary yet practical how-to, *Obvious Investing*, Mr. Eisenstein recounts in confidently vague detail his journey to financial gurudom, growing from appointed team leader on an internet investing project in Ms. Hermes's eighth-grade computer class to financial whiz kid in only seven days. To add to this impressive feat, two of those days took place on a weekend when, as he notes in the book, "I didn't even have to think about stocks. So I basically didn't."

His fans and longtime readers should not expect the madcap hilarity, danger, or utter confusion of his previous well-known works in the comic book milieu. (As Mr. Eisenstein's mother, even I did not expect this bold new direction from the prolific writer.) No, *Obvious Investing* follows in the tradition of other authoritative guides written by other young men and women of his age, such as Alyssa Fleming's *Obvious Etiquette: The Art of Being Nice to Everyone Unless They're Your Parents* and Colin Watts's *Obvious Dating: Just Butt Out, Dad.* Mr. Eisenstein's voice in *Obvious Investing*, a fresh take on the genre's typical annoyed world-weariness, is a towering monument to financial wisdom and inexplicable understatement.

"This is a required addition to the modern Wall Street bible canon," states his Uncle Dave, who played Dave on season two, episode four of *Dog with a Blog*. With startling accuracy, distinctly unburdened by any life experience or conscientious objections, Henry predicts wealth-generating winners, including the following:

- Phillip Morris
- Oil
- McDonalds
- Bonds, I guess

For the first time, Mr. Eisenstein reveals his trade secrets for getting ahead, such as tricking your ~~classmates~~ fellow investors into putting the entirety of their meager allotted funds on dumb stuff like radio stations and cryptocurrency so that *you* can gain the most points with your smart picks and, therefore, take all the money. This strategy is based on part A of the "Henry Doctrine," which posits that if you can cause other people to make less money, you will obviously make more money. And, as he astutely illuminates in part B, "If a stock made money yesterday, it probably will today." Sage observations like that are de rigueur from this relative newcomer to the international money-hustling game.

Playing the stock market has never been so fun. Or simple. Like, really simple. You actually won't believe how easy it is to be a better investor than pretty much everyone else. Just don't be an overhyped, tech IPO–obsessed idiot like Jason or Manuel and you could get an A+ in being rich. Invest obviously with Henry!

DAVID BASON (@davidbason) is a music manager from California.

Foreword to Ronald Bartel's *The Bachelor's DIY Guide to Lightning Rod Assembly*

By "Ronald Bartel"

A S THE FOLLOW-UP to my previous book—which unexpectedly became the definitive how-to guide to getting out of a New York City apartment lease—my publisher asked if I would contemplate succeeding 2016's *Indoor BBQing Cookbook* with another instructional manual. How could I possibly give my publisher what he wanted? This man is cruel. I'm convinced he has no soul. My life has been an absolute disaster since people started setting "accidental" fires in their pieds-à-terre. It's been an endless thread of lawsuits and court appearances. I refused to write the *How to Tie a Perfect Hangman's Noose* book he pitched me, but he actually said he hopes to create a little franchise, and "we have to strike while the iron is hot." And evidently, the prick was serious!

Initially, I didn't know where to start recreating what happened last year. Lightning only strikes once, I thought—thank God. Then I realized, there might be an idea there . . .

My publisher wrote me yesterday saying that he's reached out to several respected authors about contributing a foreword, but, "You may have burned some bridges—get it?" (Who does this guy think he is, a stand-up comedian?) "Anywho, no one will return my calls, so you'll just have to write your own." Again, evidently, he was serious, because here we are with a foreword by yours truly.

Before you get into my new book, I wanted to use this as an opportunity to clear some things up about *The Indoor BBQing Cookbook*.

The resulting audience for the cookbook was *not at all* the one I intended to reach. I really did put a lot of effort into those recipes, you know—the smoked brisket with burnt ends is to die for. Why is no one talking about the recipes? Why does it all have to be about loopholes and lawyers?

I've struggled and starved for years trying to make it as a writer. This is not at all how I expected my big break to come. I never thought I'd end up on the talk show circuit. I mean, I hoped for a little press, maybe a little community public television with an easy cooking demo before the weather guy's segment . . . I didn't mean for any of this to happen this way.

I did not mean for people to take my cookbook so literally. (Kids say that all the time these days—"literally." "My boss *literally* ripped my head off." "I *literally* might starve to death if I don't get my lunch break right now." Listen, you little punk, you don't know what hungry is. I'm an old man eating stewed tomatoes from a can!) I just wanted you to know that if you were *really* in a pinch, you could whip up a couple things with some basic household items. I had no idea it would lead to such destruction, and I'm sorry, OK?

Well, I need the damn money to cover my legal fees, so here we are. I hate my publisher. Thanks for buying the book, yada yada, and whatever the hell else you want to put in here.

Here it is, at long last . . . *The Bachelor's DIY Guide to Lightning Rod Assembly.*

Ronald Bartel, reluctantly successful legal adviser

HANNAH LINDOFF is a children's book author, marketing executive, and mother of three. Her work has been published in *Spider* magazine and on Offbeathome.com.

Foreword to Shadree Ivancovich's
Digging Mommyhood

By "Dr. Sarah Schist, PhD"

WHEN MY BEST FRIEND and *Arctic Gold Diggers* cast mate Shadree Ivancovich (née Buckley) asked me to write the foreword to her parenting book, *Digging Mommyhood*, I couldn't have been more thrilled. No, I haven't seen her in a while, but we've always been an unlikely team: me, a professional geologist and her, a professional party planner; both of us part of a cohort of young women heading out into the permafrost, misled to believe we were to compete against one another for a rich husband. The show was made in the tradition of reality TV classics like *Joe Millionaire* and *I Wanna Marry "Harry"*—though, as you no doubt know, this series' charming twist was that there actually *was* no guy, and we were competing for gold and resources à la *Survivor*. I'm still not sure what these ladies thought the pickaxes were for at first, but it made for good television. And while *Gold Diggers* did not bring me fame or fortune (other than the now-infamous incident preceding my elimination from the show), it did introduce me to Shadree.

I've never had many friends. But the bond she and I formed was tighter than gold and sulfur melting together due to underground sources of hot water and pressure. Shadree loves jokes like that, about gold and the best places to find it.

I was not surprised to hear that Shadree's book of parenting tips was green-lighted even though she only just had her first baby (and some of us, who have completed our PhDs, still desperately seek publication). Because this girl can do anything! And I, for one, am happy to see her putting so much of the free advice I gave her to good use.

"Planning for Baby" is the first delightful section. If there's one thing Shadree's great at, it's planning. In fact, even when you think she's just hanging out with you as a friend, she's planning! So many good tidbits here. Can you believe after only three months of use, her Himalayan salt lamp *completely cured* her morning sickness? Maybe with nine months of intense use, electric sodium chloride might even "cure" pregnancy! At only $29.99 each, Shadree's new line of lamps are worth every penny. And I have to say, I admire her hustle. After losing my job when my elimination from *Arctic Gold Diggers* aired and was subsequently streamed worldwide, I, too, took up sales—mostly hawking the bulk of my possessions before I moved permanently to this isolated mining claim.

Do you recall Shadree's fear when she heard the wolves howling at night across the tundra, and how I tried to calm her by educating her about these beautiful animals? Little did I know that my stories about wolves prechewing meat and regurgitating it for their pups would inspire Shade to do the same for *her* little "pup"! The photographs included of her performing this technique were also a surprise! It's certainly fair to call this book a page-turner.

Two words: nipple confusion. I didn't know this was an issue, but after thirty-one pages on the subject, I'm pretty sure I have it!

The holiday chapter of *Digging Mommyhood* also offers a lot of fun decorating ideas for the average American who still has access to retail outlets and is not currently living off the land. You'll admire the way Shadree created mixed-media print art from little Hadree's footprints and pipe cleaners. They look just like reindeer! (I would know. A herd passes here during their annual migration.) I also loved the way the folksy narrative describes painting Hadree's bottom orange and the accompanying full-page illustration of the "pumpkin" this made for Halloween.

Yes, I, too, was surprised when Shadree chose to paint her own bottom and create a second print, but that's Shadree for you—unpredictable! I think most of us who spent significant time with Shadree without the benefit of proper ladies' room facilities might argue that there's no way that print is actually her ass. Some might even suggest she painted a couple of overinflated balloons. But the ensuing infection she describes certainly seems to have been drawn from an actual experience. As a geologist, I'd say Shadree Ivancovich could have used two five-pound bags of pea gravel to create a more realistic butt print, but this is her book of tips, not mine.

And speaking of cottage cheese, wow, 112 is a lot of uses for breast milk! Good thing Shadree's already looking for a kindergarten that will allow her to nurse during recess.

I know *Digging Mommyhood* will be a hit. I know this just like I *knew* that the grizzly stalking our campsite for several days was a man in a suit! I just want to say that once and for all. And I'm telling you, Shadree had asked me earlier to leave her and run if the grizzly charged! If the footage looks like I pushed her, you are not taking into account the ridiculous shoes she was wearing and the effects of thawing permafrost on the topography when she fell into the grizzly's paws.

Of course, I was as relieved as everyone else to discover that it happened to be nasal spray tycoon Robert Ivancovich in the suit. Not because I ever thought it was a real bear but because I've met the kind of men who live in the wilderness communing with animals! As I'm sure you saw, the two fell instantly in love (the instant after Shadree heard how much Robert is worth) and the one season wonder, *Arctic Gold Diggers,* ended up more *The Bachelor* than *Survivor,* despite the producers' intent. Ah, love!

Thank goodness it was Shadree who got my maps and sluice box after the other women called me a murderer and voted me off the show. It feels good to know that my hunch was right and that riverbed was full of gold. Not that she needs it, now that Shadree popped out that sweet ~~child support payment~~ baby girl. I expect the rich pages of *Digging Mommyhood* will keep me feeling warm and happy for a long, time—at least an hour, if I rake the coals properly.

CAT ZAMBITO is an actor, voice-over artist, and host based out of New York City. She is also a freelance writer and has written features for *Westchester Magazine*, *Westchester Weddings*, and *914INC*. She lives with her husband, three sons, a cat, and a fish. She is essentially Smurfette in a sea of smurfs.

Foreword to Edward Schwartz's *Find Your True Voice: Lessons Learned in the Life of a Working Microphone*

By Cat Zambito

VERY EARLY ON in my voice-over career I had the odd, but over-all life-changing, experience of meeting a talking microphone named Eddie.

Now, this was in 2001, before our phones and electronic devices listened to us. So imagine my shock when, in between takes in an audition for a Pepperidge Farm commercial, I heard a raspy voice blurt out, "You're not going to read it like that, are ya?" I looked around quickly but saw that no one was in the room. Was this a prank, or some strange audition technique?

I heard the voice say, "You're looking right at me." The only thing I was looking at was a microphone. "Yeah, that's right. It's me. Hello." I initially wondered if I had cracked under the pressure of the audition, but I had been auditioning for a while and it doesn't usually get to me. As odd as it was, it seemed to be real. So after some awkward introduction on my part, the beginnings of a new (and obviously strange) friendship began.

To help me get over my jitters, Eddie shared a story from when he was a child star doing voice-overs in commercials. His first big job was a Pepsi commercial with Cindy Crawford, whom he had the biggest crush on. So much so that it took two days to shoot the commercial (instead of one) because he kept messing up his lines. He didn't seem to mind, though, since he got to spend extra time with Cindy. She was really sweet about it, too, he said.

At that audition, Eddie gave me some of the best support and advice I have ever received (not just about voice-over work but also life in general). "Go with your gut, kid!" Needless to say, I got the job.

Over the years, we have worked a lot together, and we have gotten to know one another well. But even I was surprised when I read this book—Eddie hadn't told me about what happened in his early teenage years, when his voice changed and then the novelty of being a "talking microphone" wasn't such a desired novelty anymore.

As he shares in this book, he went through some dark and depressing times, breaking into recording studios he used to work with to get a good night's charging. But he pulled himself out of his despair, realized that he had a true niche in coaching others, and has now made quite a name for himself in the business. He's helped actors and voice actors catapult their careers from nothing to commercial stardom, and some have even become household names. In fact, he even coached Siri for her audition with Apple, and just look at her now! I don't think there is anyone he hasn't worked with, and I believe him when he says that he has literally heard it all.

In addition to sharing Eddie's inspiring life story and actionable life advice, this book is also full of dishy industry gossip. Imagine being the closest thing to an actual fly on the wall! I laughed out loud reading about the things he witnesses on a daily basis—for example, he divulges how George Takei always has to come in an hour before any session and sanitize the space with Clorox wipes. (Eddie says by the time George is done, he is coughing out bleach bubbles.) James Earl Jones invites him to have a whiskey (or five) and a Cuban cigar after a session, and after they are both good and drunk they recite Star Wars quotes in Darth Vader and Yoda voices. Seth Green sages himself and the studio every time he comes in, and makes Eddie say some "earthy-crunchy-smunchy voodoo crap" (his words, not mine) before they start to clear the space. Ellen DeGeneres dances around the room and they sing the whole Weird Al canon to loosen up.

One of my favorite stories, however, didn't make it into this book, and I would like to share it with you all because it's just so Eddie. After a particularly grueling day for him, a couple of the actors and I suggested we all go out and grab a drink to unwind. So we went to a nearby haunt for happy hour, and who should walk in but the one and only Meryl Streep. Eddie (who of course knows her) called her over for a shot, and we all started chatting (as naturally as we could in the presence of Hollywood royalty). Midconversation, Eddie just blurted out, "You know, sometimes I feel like you overact." The rest of us all just sat there with our mouths agape, but Meryl just took it in stride, laughed her signature laugh, and gave Eddie a peck, as if he had just given her a compliment. See, that is one of the most incredible things about him; he has the ability to be endearing while also being a little snarky. When you are so good at what you do, you can get away with anything, because people respect your work. That's another thing I learned from him.

In fact, there is so much that we can all gain from Eddie's decades of experience, brutal honesty, and charming wit. Get ready to embark on both an unusual and yet captivating journey, while gaining some interesting new perspectives along the way. Eddie doesn't hold back (as you might have noticed), but I find that refreshing. He tells it like it is . . . to *everyone*. He doesn't care if you are the doorman, Meryl Streep, or the CEO of Google; he will tell you how he feels at any given moment. Sometimes, Eddie's perspective and advice might be hard to hear. But his past has taught him that he has nothing to lose, and he can recreate himself again if need be, so why hold back?

Not to mention, he's also almost always right.

Eddie has often told me, "You can't be anything other than you are, so enjoy yourself." Everyone is always trying to be like someone else, or compare themselves to someone else (especially in this business). Not only is it impossible to be someone else, but trying to be holds you back. (I guess that particular Eddieism might seem easy to say when you are the one and only talking microphone, but he couldn't be any more right.)

So sit back and enjoy this sarcastic yet intelligent book from the most unique viewpoint I know. Get ready to laugh, cringe, cry, and learn. Eddie is an inspiration to us all, teaching us to live in our truths. To dance like no one is watching, perform like no one is judging, and sing like no one's listening—not even a sassy talking microphone.

SAMANTHA RUDDY is a comedian and writer who hails from outside Scranton, Pennsylvania, and makes a home now in Brooklyn. She has performed at the Women in Comedy Festival, Limestone Comedy Festival, and SF Sketchfest. In 2016 Samantha was named one of the "50 Funniest People in Brooklyn" by *Brooklyn Magazine*. In addition to stand-up, she is a contributing writer to CollegeHumor, Someecards, and Reductress. She charms her Twitter followers daily @samlymatters.

Foreword to Yaswei Kahn's *Con Yourself into Confidence: Overcoming Self-Doubt in Seven Simple Steps*

By Samantha Ruddy

WHEN YASWEI KAHN asked me to write the foreword for his newest work, *Con Yourself into Confidence*, I wasn't sure I was up to the task. I had a lot of questions for myself: Am I the right person for this? Does anyone care about my opinion? Can I even read?

These questions haunted me. I would wake up in the middle of the night and call my literary agent, Brenda. Brenda would reassure me by saying things like "I'm not your literary agent," and "Stop calling me." I would like to start by thanking her. This foreword would not exist without her counsel, compassion, and inability to screen calls.

There are books that come around once in a generation. Is that too dramatic? It feels like a lot. Let's try that again. This is a book in a generation. It has words in it. If you read it forward, it is a self-help book. If you read it backward, you develop crippling self-esteem issues.

Not really. But wouldn't it be wild if books worked like that?

Honestly, I'm still not sure if I was the right choice to introduce readers to this powerful book. A foreword is supposed to give readers an idea of what the book is all about. It's like the display window of a store—but for books. I have no idea how to set up a window display. That's the reason I once worked at a JCPenney's for less than an hour.

Despite my self-doubts, I must go on with the foreword. So, I will say it in four words: Buy this book now.

Will you buy it now?

You already did and that's why you're reading this?

Good, because here's four more words: I didn't read it. Yeah, that's right. I never read it. It's very long. Why is it so long? I got overwhelmed and kept reading the same sentence over and over again. I mean, *obviously*, I didn't read the book. These are not the musings of a woman who reads self-help books. Hey, that's great that you're working your shit out, though. Good for you.

Afterword

Fantasy. Creativity. Imagination. These are all words used to describe the need to write. The reason we write. The reason we need to tell a story.

Our imagination propels us to find that fantastical story deep within us and create a world into which we can escape. We wrestle it out from our minds and into our hands and onto the page . . . words able to conjure up the beasts we've created. And once released, they live in the minds and hearts of all those who find our pages . . . changing their thoughts along the way. Shaping and molding young and old . . . thoughts and ideas never to be dismissed or silenced again.

Sometimes those stories are based in fact. Sometimes those stories are based in fiction. And sometimes, they are both, bending and twisting the truth so that no one knows what is real and what is not. Like this book you just read . . . you just had to go along for the ride without looking around to get your bearings. That is the power of the storyteller—convincing the reader to join in, even if it's a stretch of the imagination.

In this book you read forewords to books that don't exist, but truth and fiction were still intertwined. Where the power of the creative mind blurs the lines of reality, it leaves you asking, "What if?"

As lovers of books, we find many ways to celebrate writers' great creativity. We recently spent a few weeks at the sixteenth-century villa of the great political philosopher Niccolò Machiavelli, where we dined in rooms that once housed the Machiavelli family, walked along the grounds where he created *The Prince*, and sipped wine under the frescos that Michelangelo painted for him all those centuries ago. While we were there, we held toasts to Niccolò and his great *letteratura* and spent time in his former cottage imagining him at his desk writing. Writing ideas that would shape the world. What if we had been there? What would he think of the politics of today? Would he let us read his draft? What would we say? Would he ask our opinion? What if?

And maybe, just maybe, he would ask us to write his foreword.

Chazz and Gianna Palminteri

Acknowledgments, Thank-Yous, and the Like

By Jon Chattman

‿

Foreword by Denis Hurley

S o, Jon Chattman wrote a book.

Well, how do you like that?

As a matter of fact, he apparently wrote at least a coupla books, not that I heard about any of that from him.

I can't tell you *exactly* how I heard about the publications, but over the years I've made some friends in the British intelligence agencies, and, as you may have read, they like to put out memos about rude, ungrateful Americans who have no respect for their elders . . . their teachers, even!

That was always the way with Jonny . . . unless he needed something from you.

I remember the first day Jonny came to my journalism class. He and these three other yahoos were all whooping and talking about baseball until this young woman, who was no doubt reacting to the September heat wave, showed up in very, very short white shorts.

That shut them up.

When I got to know them better, I realized that was probably the highlight of their educational careers.

But enough about him. These clandestine sources I told you about got me a prepublication proof of his acknowledgment chapter to this new book.

Guess who isn't in it?

Hint: his name begins with Professor, some would say, "Iconic Professor." Some would say, "Changed-My-Life-Completely Professor." A few even have said, "Unequalled-in-the-History-of-Professing Professor."

But Jonny, hah! He says nothing. Nada. Zilch.

You did it all on your own, right Jonny? Big Author Jonny, who didn't know a gerund from an umlaut when he first showed up in my class. Big Writer Jonny, who begged me to put a lot of crap in a recommendation letter so he could get his first job.

Hah!

You think I'm bitter? You're damn right I'm bitter. And this is only the first shot. I'm starting a smear campaign that'll make him wish he were Attila the Hun and Blackbeard the Pirate rolled into one.

Just you wait, Jonny Big Shot. The truth is getting ready to sneak up and bite you in the butt.

And one old man is gonna enjoy every minute of it.

DENIS M. HURLEY is a professor of journalism, former *Boston Herald* copyeditor and writer, and currently is principal of Arguendo Financial and Economic Consulting. I guess I thank him for writing this.

Acknowledgments

This book has been a labor of love. The idea came nearly six years ago, and many have helped me along the way—whether by directly supporting me on this project or just helping to give me a proverbial high five when I needed it. So with that . . . I'd like to thank so many sources of inspiration.

I want to thank my sons, Noah and Zachary. Know no matter what I do in life, and no matter how many times my eyes are glued to a device, you come first. Your smiles, laughter, and wisdom light up the darkest days and make the brightest ones even brighter. My life truly began the day I became a father, and I'm proud to be your dad. I'm also pretty psyched I got you both into Star Wars. BB-8 will always be "Baby 8" to me. R2-D2 will always be "RD2," and Darth Vader will forever be known as "Star Vader" thanks to you. To Lila Rose, the new kid on the block, welcome to the jungle—I mean, the party!

I would like to thank my wife, Alison, for being the stable one in our relationship. (Ha!) She's a dedicated teacher who works tirelessly for her students, and at home, a mother who immerses our children with insurmountable, unconditional love.

I must thank all the contributors in this book for their creativity, generosity, and in many cases, friendship. I couldn't have made this book without you. Literally. Like, I literally couldn't have. I'd especially like to single out Rainn Wilson for not only writing a killer foreword but sharing the concept with some pals of his. Class act, that fella. I'd like to thank my longtime bud, the great John Oates, from whom I'm honored to have another foreword for a book of mine (and this time, it has nothing to do with his mustache). I'd like to thank loyal people like Jeff Pearlman, Al Snow, Bronson Arroyo, Bill Lee, Jeffrey Reddick, and others who never forgot who I was after years gone by.

I would like to thank all the agents, managers, and publicists who helped me along the way—the ones who kept their promises and delivered *and* the ones who didn't. You just made me more driven. I'd like to single out Laurie Barnett for all her efforts. Cheers to BJ Mendelson, Rob Barnett, Valentina Osorio, Gianna Palminiteri, Adam Zimmer, Allegra Cohen, Erika Tooker, Rey Roldan, Cat Zambito, and Regina DeCicco, who were all awesome for helping with this project in some way. Thanks to Thomas Neumann for his Springer blessing. Special thanks to my "co-counselor" in life, Allie Tarantino. I may not have a "Wood" shirt, but I did wear sneakers to my first banquet.

I would especially like to thank Glenn, Claire, Leah, and the entire BenBella Books team for believing in this meta book concept, and for working with me before, during, and after the "A-List" phase.

I'd like to thank my family and friends, who help me drown out the outside noise of cell phone and digital device dependency, a world in chaos, and an industry whose cast of characters often makes it all feel thankless. I'd like to thank my parents, Gary and Patti, for making me the person and parent I am today, and for loving and spoiling *my* kids rotten. I'd like to single out my mom, in particular, for showing me firsthand what it means to be a caring, genuinely good-hearted person who feels deeply and loves endlessly. I'd like to thank my mother-in-law, Barbara, for caring for my boys with bottomless patience and love. I'm thankful for my sister, Alissa, even though she texts too much, but she cares as much as she taps on her keypad. I'm going to namedrop my nephew Ryan here, too, because he's pretty cool.

I'm blessed with many friends who are a source of strength for me. Thank you to Dante Mercadante, Keith Troy, Kyle Bensen, Rich "Contra Codes" Tarantino, Aishling Quinn, Deb Ryan, and quite simply Plotkin. Shout-outs go to Oren Phillips, Joe Marcello, and

Mike Farah as well, just because I love them no matter how much time passes without seeing them.

There are so many people you come across in life whom you forget to thank for the impact they've had in your life for one reason or another. So, just simply, I'm going to list some who I appreciate(d) and have helped me become a better person, have had a lasting legacy, or have made me really learn to value myself. Some are here and some are gone, but they remain an inspiration. I will always remember Stephen Spruck, Billy Ray Briley, Mark Hogg, Rosalie Kaufman, and Harvey Kaufman. I was blessed to know, work with and befriend Carol Shiffman, a person who taught me how to lead by example. She made me believe in myself because she believed in me. I aspire to be as kind, understanding, and generous a leader as she was. I will always appreciate Katie Goulart (for being a source of support and encouragement), friend-maker Jeff Ackerman, Parker Reilly, Julie Rockowitz, Liz Garger, Tina Brescia, Marco Quartero, and Merrill Harmon (and his beloved wife, Matiji). I left plenty out but felt compelled to mention those.

Off topic, or somewhat on, a few influential stars passed on while putting this book together, many of whom I pitched for this book. Three, in particular, I need to single out: I had the pleasure of interviewing Chris Cornell and Chester Bennington, and I will miss them and their music dearly. I'm pretty sure I pitched this project to the both of them because I wanted to be associated with either in some other way. I'd also like to remember Dolores O'Riordan, who shaped the musical landscape of the '90s.

I would like to dedicate this book in memory of Jimmy Snuka, and in honor of Carole Snuka. I will never forget the experience of working with the two of them on *Superfly: The Jimmy Snuka Story*. I will always consider it a career highlight, and just wish I had the chance to say goodbye to my lovely "brudda."

In closing, as Bob Marley said, "Live the life you love, love the life you live."

About the Editor

Jon Chattman has jokingly told Tom Cruise to stop hitting on his wife, enjoyed a Reuben sandwich with Randy "Macho Man" Savage, and somehow ignited Snoop Dogg to sing Dean Martin's "That's Amore." He's also asked Meryl Streep what she would do in the event of a zombie apocalypse, and she laughingly told him he stumped her. These are just some highlights in this writer/author, marketing expert, online entertainment host, talent buyer, blogger, and man-of-many-hats's career. Chattman is chief creative officer and president of Moving Forward Consulting. He has extensive background in the entertainment field, specializing in interviewing and writing about those in the music, film, and television worlds.

Chattman has authored many pop culture, sports, and wrestling-centric books, including *Time Heels* (Pitch Publishing, 2014), *How the Red Sox Explain New England* (Triumph Books, 2013), *Superfly: The Jimmy Snuka Story* (Triumph, 2012), *A Battle Royal in the Sky* (Pitch Publishing, 2012), *I Love the Red Sox, I Hate the Yankees* (Triumph, 2011), and *Sweet Stache* (Adams Media, 2009.) He's appeared on/in various publications and outlets supporting his projects, including the *Opie & Anthony Show*, the *New York Daily News*, the *New York Post*, and the *Chicago Sun-Times*, and he was mentioned on *The Howard Stern Show*.

Chattman has covered various red carpets—from the Oscars to the Indie Spirits to the Tonys—and he's interviewed an eclectic mix of celebrities, including Courtney Love, Alice Cooper, Javier Bardem, Aaron Sorkin, Hulk Hogan, Snoop Dogg, and Tracy Morgan. In August 2011, he launched an online music and entertainment series, *A-Sides*, which featured musicians performing a song or two and taking part in an informal conversation afterwards. It debuted on thisisasides.com and has appeared on the Huffington Post, *Inked* magazine, and USAtoday.com. Rising musicians and established acts who have appeared on the series include Gary Clark, Jr., Bastille, Imagine Dragons, Joe Perry, Air Supply, Letters to Cleo, The Front Bottoms, Elle King, Wyclef Jean, and Jimmy Eat World.

Chattman has written for many outlets throughout the years including the *New York Post*, *Wizard*, *Soundfly*, and *TV Guide*. He also writes band and music act bios for press purposes and websites. He formerly owned and operated *thecheappop.com*, a pop culture humor and interview site. In addition to his writing experience, Chattman promotes live music events in and around Westchester County, New York—many of which are at Garcia's in Port Chester. On two occasions, he held Pop Goes the Culture, a zany Westchester-based variety and awards show honoring all walks of pop life from the Magic Garden to Gary Gnu to Andrew W.K. He stopped because no one really attended other than friends, family, and a few glorious weirdos who "got it."

Chattman was selected as one of the "Rising Stars—Westchester's Forty Under Forty" by The Business Council of Westchester in 2011. He is currently chief creative officer at Moving Forward Consulting, a small social media and marking firm. He resides in Westchester County, New York, with his wife, Alison, and three young children. His hobbies include binge watching Netflix shows, going to the movies, Star Wars, the beach, listening to Bon Iver and pre–*Everything Now* Arcade Fire, and he is trying desperately to sever his phone from his hand. Send help.